Miss

ICELAND

BY THE SAME AUTHOR

Butterflies in November

Hotel Silence

Miss
ICELAND

Auður Ava
Ólafsdóttir

Translated from the Icelandic
by Brian FitzGibbon

Black Cat
New York

Miss Iceland was first published as *Ungfrú Ísland* by Benedikt in Iceland in 2018

First published in English in the UK by Pushkin Press in 2020

Published simultaneously in Canada
Printed in the United States of America

First Grove Atlantic paperback edition: June 2020

ISBN 978-0-8021-4923-7
eISBN 978-0-8021-4924-4

Designed and typeset by Tetragon, London

Library of Congress Cataloging-in-Publication data is available for this title.

Black Cat
an imprint of Grove Atlantic
154 West 14th Street
New York, NY 10011

Distributed by Publishers Group West

groveatlantic.com

20 21 22 23 24   10 9 8 7 6 5 4 3 2 1

In memory
of my parents

*There are, it may be, so many kinds of voices in the world,
and none of them is without significance.*

(FIRST EPISTLE OF PAUL THE APOSTLE
TO THE CORINTHIANS)

*One must still have chaos within oneself, to give birth to a
dancing star.*

(NIETZSCHE, *THUS SPOKE ZARATHUSTRA*)

CONTENTS

Nothing is still or dead in the entrails of the earth, for that is where the most powerful and menacing of the elements rages, and that is fire.

(JÓNAS HALLGRÍMSSON,
FJÖLNIR LITERARY JOURNAL, 1835)

1942

The room of the one who gave birth to me

I stumbled across an eagle's nest when I was five months pregnant with you, a two-metre rough cavity of flattened lyme-grass on the edge of a cliff by the river. Two pudgy eaglets were huddled up inside it. I was alone and an eagle circled above me and the nest. It flapped its wings heavily, one of which was tattered, but refrained from attacking. I assumed it was the female. She followed me all the way to the edge of the farm, a black shadow looming over me like a cloud that obscured the sun. I sensed the baby would be a boy and decided to name him Örn—Eagle. On the day you were born, three weeks before your time, the eagle flew over the farm again. The old vet that had come to inseminate a cow was the one who delivered you; his final official duty before retiring was to deliver a baby. When he came out of the cow shed, he took off his waders and washed his hands with a new bar of Lux soap. Then he lifted you into the air and said:

"Lux mundi.

"Light of the world."

Although he was accustomed to allowing the female to lick its offspring unassisted, he started to fill the blood-pudding mixing tub to bathe you. I saw him roll up the sleeves of his flannel shirt and dip an elbow into the water. I watched them—the vet and your father—stoop over you with their backs to me.

3

"She's her father's daughter," your father said. Then he added and I clearly heard him: "Welcome, Hekla dear."

He had already decided on the name without consulting me.

"Not a volcano, not the gateway to hell," I protested from the bed.

"These gateways have to be allowed to be somewhere on this earth," I heard the vet say.

The men pressed together to hunch down over the tub again and took advantage of my defencelessness, my aching pain.

I didn't know when I got married that your father was obsessed with volcanoes. He would submerge himself in books with descriptions of volcanic eruptions, correspond with three geologists, have foreboding dreams about eruptions, live in the constant hope of seeing a plume of smoke in the sky and feel the earth tremble under his feet.

"Perhaps you'd like the earth to crack open at the bottom of our field?" I asked. "For it to split in two like a woman giving birth?"

I hated lava fields. Our farmland was surrounded on all sides by thousand-year-old lava fields that had to be clambered over to go pick blueberries; you couldn't stick a fork into a single potato patch without striking a rock.

"Arnhildur, the female eagle," I say from under the cover that your father pulls over me. "The one who is born to wage battles. There are barely twenty eagles living in this country, Gottskálk, I add, but more than two hundred volcanoes." That was my last card.

"I'll make you a nice cup of coffee," your father said. That was his compromise. He had made up his mind. I turned the other way and shut my eyes, I wanted to be left in peace.

Four and a half years after you were born, Hekla erupted after its one-hundred-and-two-year slumber. That's when your father finally got to hear the roaring explosion he had been pining to hear in the west in the Dalir district, like the distant echo of the recently ended world war. Your brother Örn was two years old at the time. Your father immediately called his sister in the Westman Islands to find out what she could see through the kitchen window. She was frying crullers and said that a plume of volcanic smoke hovered over the island, that the sun was red and that it was raining ash.

He covered the mouthpiece and repeated every single sentence to me.

"She says that the sun is red and it's raining ash and that it's as dark as night and she had to turn the lights on."

He wanted to know if it was a spectacular and daunting sight and if the floor was shaking.

"She says it's a spectacular and daunting sight and that all the drainpipes are full of ash and that her husband, the boat mechanic, is up on a ladder trying to unclog them."

He lay with his ear glued to the radio and gave me the highlights.

"They say that the mouth of the volcano, the crater, is shaped like a heart, a heart of flames." Or he said: "Steinthóra, did you know that one of the lava bombs was eleven metres long and five metres wide and shaped like a cigar?"

Eventually he could no longer satisfy himself with his sister's descriptions of the views from her kitchen window or the frozen black-and-white photographs of the giant pillar of smoke on the front page of the Tíminn newspaper. He longed to see the eruption with his own eyes, he wanted to see colours, he wanted to see glowing blocks of lava, whole boulders shooting into the air, he wanted to see the red fiery eyes spitting shooting stars like sparks in a foundry, he wanted to see a black lava wall crawling forward like an illuminated metropolis, he wanted to know if the flames of the volcano turned the sky pink, he wanted to feel the heat on his eyelids, he wanted his eyes to tingle, he wanted to charge down south to Thjórsárdalur in his Russian jeep.

And he wanted to take you with him.

"Jónas Hallgrímsson, our national poet, who produced the best alliterations and poetry about volcanoes ever written, never witnessed an eruption," he said. "Neither did the naturalist Eggert Ólafsson. Hekla can't miss seeing her namesake erupting."

"Why don't you just sell the farm and move down south to become a farmer in Thjórsárdalur instead?" I asked. I could just as easily have asked: "Don't you want to move from the land of Laxdæla Saga to the Land of Njál's Saga?"

He sat you on a cushion on the passenger seat of the jeep so that you could see the view, and I was left behind with your brother Örn to take care of the farm. When he returned with melted soles on his boots, I knew he had gone too close.

"The old dear's arteries are still bubbling," he said, and carried you to bed, sleeping in his arms.

In the summer, ash reached us in the west in Dalir and destroyed the fields.

Dead animals were found in troughs where gas puddles had formed: foxes, birds and sheep. Then your father finally stopped talking about volcanoes and went back to farming. You, however, had changed. You had been on a journey. You spoke differently. You spoke in volcanic language and used words like sublime, magnificent and ginormous.

You had discovered the world above and looked up at the sky. You started to disappear and we found you out in the fields, where you lay observing the clouds; in the winter, we found you out on a mound of snow, contemplating the stars.

I

MOTHERLAND

Who has a fairer fatherland,
With mountains, valleys, blackened sand,
Northern lights in a glowing band
and slopes of birch and brook?

(HULDA, 1944)

1963

Poets are men

The dust hovers in a cloud behind the Reykjavík coach, the road is a ridged washboard and we rattle on; bend after bend, soon it becomes impossible to see through the muddy windows and, before long, the *Laxdæla Saga* trail will vanish into the dirt.

The gearstick creaks every time the driver goes up or down a hill; I suspect the coach has no brakes. The large diagonal crack across the windscreen doesn't seem to bother the driver. There aren't many cars about and, on the rare occasions when we meet one, the driver blows his horn. To make room for a road grader, the bus needs to swerve over to the side of the road where it teeters. The levelling of Dalir's roads is regarded as something of an event, giving the driver an opportunity to wind down his window, lean out and have a lengthy chat.

"I'll be lucky if I don't lose a spindle," I hear the bus driver say.

Right now I'm not a short distance away from the village of Búðardalur, but actually in Dublin, since my finger is stuck on page twenty-three of *Ulysses*. I'd heard of this novel that was as thick as Njál's Saga and could

15

be bought from the English bookshop in Hafnarstræti and sent west.

"Is it French you are talking, sir?" the old woman said to Haines.
Haines spoke to her again a longer speech, confidently.
"Irish," Buck Mulligan said. "Is there Gaelic on you?"
"I thought it was Irish," she said, "by the sound of it."

The reading was proceeding slowly, both because of the shaking of the bus and because my English is poor. Even though I have a dictionary lying on the empty seat beside me, the language is more challenging than I expected.

I peer through the window. Didn't a female writer live on that farm? Didn't the strong current of this coal-grey river full of sand and mud ripple through her veins? She made the cattle suffer, people said, because while she sat writing about the love lives and tragic fates of the locals, striving to transform the sheep's colours into a sunset over Breidafjördur, she neglected to milk the cows. There was no greater sin than forgetting to empty swollen udders. Whenever she visited a neighbouring farm, she sat for too long and either wanted to recite a poem or fell silent for hours on end, dipping her sugar cubes into the coffee. They say she heard a string orchestra when she wrote and also that she woke up her children in the night and carried them out into the farmyard in her arms to show them the shimmering waves of Northern Lights undulating across the black sky, and that in between these periods she locked herself inside the marital bedroom and pulled a quilt over her head. There was so much melancholy in her that one bright spring evening she vanished into the silvery grey depths of the river. The prospect of eating fresh puffin eggs would no longer do her, because she had stopped sleeping. She was found in a trout net by the bridge and dragged onto the banks: a stiff-winged poet in a soaking wet skirt and laddered stockings, her belly full of water.

"She destroyed the net," said the farmer who owned it. "I placed it there for trout, but the meshwork wasn't designed to hold a woman poet."

Her fate served as a warning, but at the same time she was the only model of a female author I had.

Otherwise poets were men.

I learnt from that not to disclose my plans to anyone.

Radio Reykjavík

Sitting in front of me on the coach is a woman travelling with a little girl who needs to throw up again. The coach swerves on the gravel and halts. The driver presses a button and the door opens to the autumn air, hissing like a steam iron. The weary woman dressed in a woollen coat escorts the girl down the steps. This is the third time the car-sick child has to be let out. The roads are lined with ditches because the farmers are draining the land and drying up the wetlands where wading birds nest. Barbed wire fences protrude from the earth here and there, although it is difficult to make out what property they are supposed to delimit.

Soon I'll be too far away from home to know the names of the farms. On the steps, the woman shoves a woolly hat over the child's head and yanks it down over her ears. I watch her holding the girl's forehead as a thin streak of vomit oozes out of her. Finally she digs into a coat pocket, pulls out a handkerchief and wipes the child's mouth before hoisting her back onto the dust-filled coach.

I dig out my notebook, uncap my fountain pen and write two sentences. Then I put the cap back on and open *Ulysses* again.

The driver bangs his pipe empty on the steps, turns on the radio, and the men move to the front of the bus, broad shoulders and hats huddle together to listen. The weather forecast and announcements are about to begin. The driver turns up the volume to drown out the rattle of the engine. *Hello, this is Radio Reykjavík* is heard, then crackling and he turns the knob to find the right wavelength. The sound is bad and I hear that they are looking for a sailor on a boat. Ready to weigh anchor. Then there is a hiss and the speaker is cut off. The men spread around the bus again and light cigarettes.

I turn the page. Stephen Dedalus is drinking tea as the coach driver overtakes the Ferguson tractor that had passed us when the child was throwing up. *Stephen filled a third cup, a spoonful of tea colouring faintly the thick rich milk.*

How many pages would it take to overtake the tractor if James Joyce were a passenger on the coach to Reykjavík?

Mother whales

The last stop is at the diner in Hvalfjördur where a boat is pulling in with two sperm whales. They're tied to either side of the gunwale, each whale exceeding the length of the boat, sea foam swirling over their black carcasses. The vessel sways in the breaking waves; compared to the giant mammals, it looks like a flimsy toy floating in a bathtub. The driver is the first to abandon the bus, followed by the passengers. A pungent stench wafts from the boiling pots of blubber and the travellers scurry into the diner. They're selling asparagus soup and breaded chops with potatoes and rhubarb jam, but I haven't got a job yet and I have to watch my spending, so I buy a cup of coffee and slice of pound cake. On my way back to the coach, I pick two handfuls of blueberries.

At the whaling station, a middle-aged man joins the group of passengers. He's the last one to step on the coach, surveys the group, spots me and wants to know if the seat beside me is free. I move the dictionary and he tips his hat slightly as he sits. When the coach drives off, he lights a cigar.

"All we need now is some dessert," he says. "What one wouldn't do for a box of darn Anthon Berg chocolates."

He popped over to Hvalfjördur to visit an acquaintance who owns all the frigging whales in the sea, he says, and they ate some chops together.

"They've carved up five hundred whales this summer. No wonder Icelanders call the smell of shit the smell of money." Then he turns to me.

"Might I ask you for your name, miss…?"

"Hekla."

"How perfectly befitting. *Hekla doth rise high and sharp to the heavens.*"

He examines the book I am holding.

"And you read foreign books?"

"Yes."

One of the sperm whales has been dragged up a concrete slipway into the carving yard, where it lies in one piece, a giant black carcass as big as the Dalasýsla Savings Bank back home. Bare-handed young men in waders and jeans immediately attack the beast, brandishing giant blades in the air, and are already busy flensing the blubber and fat off the whale, steel glistening in the autumn sun. Soon the youths are covered in liver oil. The entrails lie scattered by the creature's side, as a flock of birds swarms above them. It is obviously difficult for the young men to walk on the slippery platform by the try pots.

"I see, is the girl checking out the boys?" asks the man. "Doesn't a sweet girl like you have a boyfriend?"

"No."

"What, aren't all the lads chasing after you? Is no one poking you?"

I open the book and continue reading without the dictionary. Some moments later the man picks up the conversation again.

"Did you know that it's forbidden to harpoon a mother whale, which is why the lads only butcher the males?"

He stubs out his cigar in the ashtray on the back of the seat.

"Unless it's by accident," he adds.

We drive past the military barracks and oil tanks of the American army and two armed soldiers standing on the road wave at us. The road twists on up the mountain and even more scree lies ahead. Finally a view of the capital across the strait opens up under a pink evening sky; perched on the peak of a barren mound of rock is a half-finished church dedicated to a poor author of psalms. The tower with its scaffolding can be seen all the way from Kjós.

I close the book.

On a side road down Mosfellsdalur, we meet a car and the coach driver suddenly slows down.

"Isn't that our Nobel Prize winner?" a man is heard asking as the passengers stir and peer through the muddy windows.

21

"If that's a four-door Buick Special model 1954, then it's him all right," says the driver. "Fantastic suspension and powerful heater," he adds.

"Doesn't he have a green Lincoln now?" asks another man.

The men aren't so sure any more and even think they might have seen a woman at the wheel and children in the backseat.

By then I had been sitting on the bus and chewing dust for eight hours.

In the last hour:
Reykjavík, foggy, slight drizzle

I'm standing on the lot of the BSÍ coach terminal in Hafnarstræti and waiting for the driver to hand me my case along with my other parcels from the roof. Night is falling and the shops have closed, but I know that Snæbjörn Bookstore, which sells English books, is nearby. Feeling shivery after the journey, I adjust the scarf around my throat and button up my coat. My neighbour from the bus sidles up to me and tells me that it just so happens that he sits on the board of the Reykjavík Beauty Society along with some acquaintances of his, including the owner of the whales in the sea. The society's objective is to embellish the city and promote good taste and decorum among the population, which is why, for a number of years now, it has

22

been hosting a beauty contest. It was initially held in the Tivoli amusement park in Vatnsmýri, but has now actually been moved indoors.

"We can't allow rain forecasts to postpone our contest every year. Apart from which the ladies caught colds outside.

"…No, the thing is," I hear the man continue, "we're looking for unattached maidens, sublimely endowed with both clean-limbedness and comeliness to take part in the competition. I can recognize beauty when I see it, and I would therefore like to invite you to participate in Miss Iceland."

I size up the man.

"No, thank you."

The man won't give in.

"All your features curve and sway like an Icelandic summer's day."

He digs into his jacket pocket, pulls out a card and hands it to me. It contains his name and phone number. *Tradesman*, it says after his name.

"Should you change your mind."

He ponders a moment.

"You're darn pretty in those plaid slacks."

Mokka

I walk away with my case and head towards a basement flat in Kjartansgata. The clock on the quadrilateral tower in

23

Lækjartorg shows close to seven. On one of its sides is the picture of a smiling woman in a sleeveless pale-blue dress with a wide skirt, who is holding a box of Persil washing powder. In the square, two women in brown woollen coats sit on a wooden bench with iron armrests, while seagulls peck at some breadcrumbs nearby.

I walk up Bankastræti, which is lined with multi-coloured cars, American hot wheels with leather-upholstered seats. The guys are out prowling and blow their horns, with their elbows leaning out the windows, cigarettes dangling from their mouths and brilliantined hair, slowly accosting me, barely older than kids. There are even more bookshops than I had dared to imagine, I also pass a tobacconist's, a men and women's clothing store and Lárus G. Lúdvíksson's shoe shop. To shake off the cars I turn up Skólavördustígur.

There's Mokka, the café where all the Reykjavík poets hang out, known back home as those smartarse losers who live down south and lounge about in public places drinking coffee all day. I linger a moment outside the window, case in hand, and peer into the thick smoke; the interior is dark and I can't make out any of the poets' faces.

Kjartansgata

The doorbell is labelled *Lýdur and Ísey* and below this is a *bell out of order* sign. A pram is parked beside the basement door. The fence has fallen into disrepair and in front of the house is a patch of unkempt grass.

I knock. Ísey, my childhood friend, opens the door and smiles from ear to ear. She is wearing a green skirt, and her hair is cut short and held back by a headband.

She embraces me and drags me inside.

"I've been looking forward to you coming to town all summer," she says.

A baby sits on a rug on the floor, banging two wooden blocks together.

She whisks her daughter off the mat and rushes over to me with her. The girl isn't happy to let go of the blocks. Ísey pulls the dummy out of her mouth, kisses her wet cheek and introduces us. A trail of saliva dangles from the dummy.

"Let me introduce you to Thorgerdur," she says. "Thorgerdur, this is Hekla, my best friend."

She hands me the child. She's the spitting image of her father.

The baby wriggles in my arms and blows a raspberry at me.

My friend takes the child back and places her on the floor, and then embraces me again and wants to show me around the flat.

"I'm so happy to see you, Hekla. Tell me what you're reading. I've no time to read. I've such a longing for it. I'm lucky if I manage to read two poems before I fall asleep. I have a card for the library in Thingholtsstræti, but I've got no one to babysit for me while I fetch the books."

The child has lost interest in the blocks and wiggles off the rug. She tries to hoist herself to her feet by grabbing onto a lamp stand, which wobbles. Her mother grabs her and sticks the dummy back into her mouth. She spits it straight out again.

"It's so much work being with a small child, Hekla. We're together all week, all day long and also at night when Lýdur is away doing road work in the east. I didn't know it would be so wonderful to be a mother. Having a baby has been the best experience of my life. I'm so happy. There's nothing missing in my life. Your letters have kept me alive. I'm so lonely. Sometimes I feel like I'm a terrible mother. Then my mind is elsewhere when Thorgerdur is trying to attract my attention. I'm so scared of something happening to her. You can never let a child out of your sight. Not even when I'm folding nappies. She might stick something into her mouth. The best time of the day is when Thorgerdur is asleep in her pram in the morning and I make some coffee and read *Tíminn*. I read my coffee grounds every day. There are no deaths. I look forward to when Thorgerdur will be a teenager and we can discuss books together. Like you and I used to do. That's another twelve years away. Thorgerdur's had a cold and is peevish and sleeps with me, but when Lýdur comes home at the weekends, he wants her to sleep in her own bed. We slip on an Ellý Vilhjálms record and dance. He's thinking of quitting his job at the Road Administration. We're saving up to buy a small patch of land in Sogamýri. Lýdur wants a garage to start his own upholstering or framing company. He says you can also make a packet stuffing birds. Unless he gets a job at the cement factory, then we'll move to Akranes. A new family moved into the basement next door last month. Lýdur lent a hand and helped carry a dresser. They didn't have much furniture. I just caught a glimpse of her. I think she's about our age and she has four kids. The youngest is around the same age as my Thorgerdur. It's been five weeks since they moved in and there aren't any curtains in the living room yet. When I got up last night and drank a glass of milk at the kitchen window and I looked out into the darkness, I noticed that the woman was also standing by her kitchen window and looking into the darkness too. I felt she looked really glum. I saw myself reflected in the window and the woman was also reflected in her window, two sleepless women, and for a moment our mirrored images fused and I felt as if she were standing in my kitchen and I in hers, can you imagine anything so silly? The only man I talk to during the day is the fishmonger. There are two of them as it happens. Twins and they work in shifts. I only realized it yesterday when they were in the store at the same time and stood side by side. It was difficult to tell them apart. Then I understood why the fishmonger sometimes jokes with me and calls me his darling and sometimes not; it's because it's not the same guy. They wrap the fish in newspaper, *Morgunbladid*. Let me have a poem or a short story, I say to the guy who's serving me, no obituaries or death notices. When I got home yesterday, I carefully unwrapped the haddock in the sink, the innermost sheet was soaking and difficult to read but on the next page, there were two poems by a poet who sits in Café Mokka all day long. Sorry if I blab too much. Are you going to go to Mokka and Laugavegur 11 to sit with the poets? I've walked past there with the pram and seen them hunched over their coffee cups, lacing them with liquid that comes out of brown paper bags. The waitresses turn a blind eye to it. What would happen if I strolled into the cloud of smoke with Thorgerdur in my arms and ordered a cup of coffee? Or walked into an abstract art exhibition in Bogasalur with the pram?"

"You could give it a try."

She shakes her head.

"You wear trousers and go your own way, Hekla."

The child is tired and rests her head on my friend's shoulder as she paces the floor with her a few times. Then she says she's going to put her daughter to sleep while I have a look around.

That's quickly done.

There is very little furniture in the small living room: a green plush sofa and a sideboard against the wall with a crocheted tablecloth and three photographs in gilded frames: a wedding shot of Ísey with a beehive hairdo, a picture of a baby and finally, one of me and Ísey. I bend over to examine it. We stand smiling by a stone sheepfold,

I in bib overalls, wool sweater and my brother Örn's waders, which are three sizes too big for me, having just chased after two ewes all day in the canyon. Ísey hadn't joined in the search, but helped the women to butter rye pancakes, fry crullers and heat cocoa in a thirty-litre pot in the catering tent. She's got brown curls, is wearing a skirt and a buttoned cardigan and is leaning her head on my shoulder. Who took that picture, was it Jón John?

After a short while, my friend returns with a hint of sleep in her eyes and quietly leans on the door behind her. I think I heard her singing the same ancient lullaby that a mother sang to her child before throwing it into a waterfall. Once more she tells me how glad she is to see me and sidles up beside me at the sideboard to scrutinize the photograph of us as if she were wondering who those girls are. The picture is two years old.

"I made that skirt myself from a picture in the paper," she finally says. "She ponders a moment. Jón John helped me with the pattern," she adds. Then she does the same to the wedding photograph: picks it up and examines it.

"I feel it's so weird to think that's me. That I'm a married woman in Reykjavík with a child. Lýdur was just a kid when he came west to Dalir to lay the power line and instal that row of electricity poles with the team of labourers; they lived in work huts, he had a record player and played the Shadows; he had such a beautiful voice that it didn't matter what he said, it made me weak in the knees; now he's a husband and father. It's so strange to think that Lýdur will be the last one."

I try to recall Lýdur's voice, but can't remember anything he said. Whenever we meet Ísey does the talking and he is mostly silent.

On the walls there are two large paintings that seem at odds with the spartan furnishings: one is of a mossy lava field and a glittering lake in a rocky rift and the other is of a steep mountain.

"Kjarval?" I ask.

"Yes, from my mother-in-law."

She says her father-in-law couldn't come to terms with the way the artist depicted it.

"He said that wasn't the Mt Lómagnúpur that he knew. He's been out at sea for thirty years and only wants boats on his walls, not landscapes and certainly not coloured rocks. Rocks are just bloody rocks, he says, not colours. The mother-in-law, on the other hand, doesn't want to see the sea in her living room. Her father was a sailor and drowned when she was small and she chose to live somewhere where the sea was out of sight."

"That's difficult on an island," I say.

"Not in Efstasund."

We contemplate the paintings.

"My mother-in-law met the painter when she was a cook for road labourers in the east. She thinks he's a decent enough man but agrees with her husband that he doesn't get the colours right. Lýdur says that if we had a garage we could keep the paintings there, at least one of them. Now he believes we could even get some money for them. I cried so much he didn't dare mention it again."

She seems preoccupied.

"I can't lose those paintings, Hekla. I look at them every day. There's so much light in them."

She walks over to the window and gazes into the darkness. A few withered blades of grass reach the glass.

"This is how deep I've sunk. This is how small my world has become: the view over Breidafjördur and its thousand islands and the biggest sky in the whole world has shrunk down to the size of a basement window on Kjartansgata."

"Still, at least your street is named after a character in the *Laxdæla Saga*."

She turns to me.

"I'm terrible. I haven't offered you anything. I had some rice pudding for dinner and can heat it up for you."

I tell her I've already eaten. That I had coffee and pound cake in Hvalfjördur. Nonetheless, she insists on opening a can of pears and whipping cream.

"It's Christmas when you come for a visit, Hekla."

I open my case and hand her a parcel wrapped in brown paper.

"Puffins from Dad," I say.

I follow her into the kitchen, which has a small Rafha electric cooker, a fridge and a table for two. On the way

31

she repeats how happy she is to see me. She says she'll cook the puffins at the weekend when Lýdur is back in town and sticks them in the fridge.

"I don't enjoy cooking but I'm learning. The other day I made Ora fishballs in pink sauce, but Lýdur's favourite is stockfish. My sister-in-law taught me how to make pink sauce. You use ketchup and flour."

I tell her that Jón John has offered me a room that he rents in Stýrimannastígur, while he's out at sea. "Until I get a job and can rent my own room," I add.

"Have you finished your manuscript?" she asks.

"Yes."

"And started another?"

"Yes."

"I always knew you would become a writer, Hekla.

"Do you remember when you were six and you had recently started to write and wrote in your childish handwriting in a copybook that the river moved like time? And that the water was cold and deep? That was before Steinn Steinarr wrote his 'Time and Water'."

She hesitates.

"I know Jón John is your best friend, Hekla."

"Male friend, yes," I say.

She looks me in the eye.

"I realize the child is a distraction for you, but stay with me until the weekend at least."

I think: that's three days. I can't write here.

I say: "I'll be here until the weekend."

We sit with the canned pears in dessert bowls, opposite one another at the kitchen table, and Ísey falls into a momentary silence. I feel there's something on her mind.

"I bought myself a diary the other day and have started to write in it."

She reveals this cautiously.

"That's how low I've sunk, Hekla."

I start thinking about my father's diary entries and how he deciphered the weather from the look of the glacier beyond the fjord every day; it didn't matter what the glacier looked like, it always augured ill, even a splendid glacier could bode a downpour over the swathes of grass.

"Do you write about the weather?" I ask.

She takes a deep breath.

"I write about what happens, but since so little happens I also write about what doesn't happen. The things that people don't say and don't do. What Lýdur doesn't say, for example."

She stalls.

"Because I add thoughts and descriptions to what happens, a quick trip to the store can take up many pages. I went out twice yesterday, once to the fish shop and once with the rubbish. When I walked to the fish shop with the pram, I shut my eyes and felt a slight heat on my eyelids. Is that a sun or not a sun? I asked myself, and I felt I was a part of something bigger."

She looks anxious.

"I keep the journal in the washing bucket because Lýdur wouldn't understand me wasting time on writing about things that don't exist or about things that are over.

"'What's over is over,' he says.

"Still though, last weekend when we got into bed, he said: 'Tell me what happened this evening, Ísa, that way it feels like it happened to someone else.' That was the most beautiful thing he has ever said to me. Afterwards he held me in his arms."

Ísey wraps her cardigan around herself.

"When I've finished writing in the diary, I feel like I've folded all the washing and cleaned up."

She stands up because she wants to pour some coffee and do a cup reading. She gets me to turn the cup upside down and place it on the hot plate. After a short while, she examines the cup in the light.

"There are two men in the cup," she says. "You love one and sleep with the other."

Like that Joyce

Ísey offers me the sofa under the Lómagnúpur cliffs, but before I fall asleep, I pull *Ulysses* out of my case, turn on the lamp and read a few pages under the orange-tasselled shade.

When I awaken I hear the mother and daughter pottering about in the kitchen. My friend is giving her daughter skyr, and the child smiles at me, plastered in white from ear to ear and claps her hands. There is constant wriggling, feet kicking in the air without touching the ground; she gesticulates wildly and flaps her arms against her sides, like a featherless bird trying to take to the sky, a thousand rapid movements, flickering eyes. It's blatantly clear: humans can't fly.

My friend dresses the child in overalls and slips a knitted cap onto her head and, once she has put her to sleep in the pram in the garden, wants to show me something. She leads me into the bedroom.

"I wallpapered this myself. What does the writer think?"

I laugh.

"Like it."

The room is covered in wallpaper of green leaves with big orange flowers.

"I had a sudden longing for wallpaper and Lýdur gave in to me."

She pushes the door closed behind us.

"He says he can't refuse me anything."

She pours coffee into the cups, puts the pot back on the stove and sits down.

"Tell me what you're reading, Hekla. That thick one."

"It's by a writer called James Joyce."

"How does he write?"

"Unlike any Icelandic writer. The whole novel happens within the space of a day. It's 877 pages. I haven't got very far with it," I add, "the text is so difficult."

"I see," says my friend, cutting a slice of Christmas cake and placing it on my plate.

"I feel it's best to write in my diary on the edge of dawn. While the outlines of the world are still blurred. It can take as much as six, seven pages for the light to come up in here. I imagine it's something similar with that Joyce."

My friend stands up and walks to the kitchen window. The pram is on the path outside, only the wheels are visible.

"I had a dream," I hear her say without turning. "I dreamt I was a passenger in a car that was driving down a side track home to the farm. In the middle of the track, I get out of the car and take a shortcut across the moor. On the way I walk past a corrie between two big tussocks that are full of blueberries the size of snowballs. They're heavy and juicy and they are a beautiful, glistening blue like a dead calm autumn sky. The last thing I remember is scooping up armfuls of sky-blue berries and filling a washtub in a split second. I was alone. Then I heard a bird. Now I'm scared that the berries are the babies I'll have, Hekla."

We are all the same,
fatally wounded and disorientated whales

I'm ready with my case when Davíd Jón John Johnsson comes to collect me. He doesn't want to come in or to accept a cup of coffee because he says he's still feeling the waves of seasickness in his gut, but he puts down his duffel bag to greet us. He first embraces me and grabs me tight, holding me for a long moment without saying a word, and I inhale the faint smell of slime from his hair. He has slipped a jacket over his salt-crystallized wool sweater. Then he embraces Ísey. Then he peeps into the pram with the sleeping child parked by the house wall.

"I came as soon as I stepped ashore," he says.

He is pale but his hair has grown longer since I saw him in the spring.

He is even more beautiful than before.

He slips his duffel bag over his shoulder and wants to carry my case.

I hold my typewriter.

A cold jet stream shoots down Snorrabraut, the grey sea can be faintly glimpsed at the end of the street and, beyond that, Mt Esja veiled in the mist that hovers over the strait. We follow the gravel pathway across the Hljómskálagardur park, passing the statue of Jónas Hallgrímsson in crumpled trousers. There the sailor pauses a moment, puts down his duffel bag and the case and gives me another quick hug. In front of the poet. Then we continue.

He tells me that before he went to sea he'd worked at the whaling station.

"We worked on shifts night and day, carving meat, sawing bone and boiling. I was the only one who didn't go sunbathing with the guys. When they realized I was different, I was afraid they'd shove me into a try pot.

"Still, there was another guy like me.

"I knew it as soon as I saw him.

"He knew it too.

"One evening when we had a break, we went off on a walk together.

"Nothing happened. After that he avoided me."

He runs a hand through his tuft of hair. It's shaking.

"They take such a long time to kill those giant creatures, the mortal battle can last a whole day."

After the whaling, he said he took two trips on a side trawler, *Saturnus*.

"I was seasick for the whole time," he says. "Constantly. With vomit in my throat. I couldn't sleep I was so nauseous. The smell of slime and scales was everywhere, even in my quilt and pillow. The weather was foul. I couldn't learn to rock with the waves. I slept on a top bunk and the horizon swayed up and down. It helped a bit when I covered the porthole with a curtain. I got the worst chores. My manhood was constantly put to the test. The crew were never sober, and they picked on me. I was so exhausted I couldn't lift my arms from my sides. Every day I was afraid I'd drown."

He hesitates.

"They tried to crawl up to me in bed, but because I slept with my clothes on, there was less danger of being raped.

"Then there was the whoring. They noticed I wasn't into women so they decided to man me up by buying me a hooker when we docked at Hull."

I look at my pale friend. Two swan couples swim close by on the Tjörnin Lake.

"I told them I didn't want to be unfaithful to my girl-friend."

He averts his gaze as he says this.

"I swear, Hekla, I couldn't survive another trip, I'm never stepping on that rusty raft again. I'm willing to take on any job that doesn't involve going out to sea."

He is silent for a moment.

"There was one saving grace, though. The second mate. He paints pictures of schooners when he's onshore but doesn't want anyone to know."

The subject makes me think of Ísey's father-in-law.

"Once the cook was too drunk to be woken up, so the mate sent me down to the storage room to take some lamb out of the freezer and make meat soup. The kitchen was the only place where I was left in peace.

"That was also where they hid their smuggled stash on the way home. Blaupunkt television sets, cartons of ciga-rettes and bottles of gin. In nooks inside the walls behind the pantry and in the freezer."

The moon is my closest neighbour

The path leads west to Stýrimannastígur, not far from the shipyard.

"Are you writing, Hekla?"

"Yes."

"Good."

We halt by a timber house, clad in rusty corrugated-iron. A steep wooden staircase leads up to the sailor's attic room. He sticks a key into the lock and says it's stiff.

I look around.

The room has a sleeping couch, a wardrobe in the corner, a bookshelf by the bed and a sewing machine that stands on a small table under the skylight. He says there is a communal toilet in the basement and a view of the stars through the skylight when the weather allows. He spotted the first star three weeks ago, he adds.

"Here you can write," he says, and removes the sewing machine from the table, opens the wardrobe and places it at the bottom.

I put the typewriter on the table.

He says he's already moved twice in the space of six months and at first lived in a basement flat in Adalstræti, which was regularly flooded by the spring tides. He then moved into another basement room in Hafnarstræti right opposite the police station.

"So they knew where to find me," he says, and adds

that queers are watched by the police. Sometimes a Black Maria drives past twice a day and the cops slow down to gawk through the windows. Kids also peeped in to spot Sodom and sometimes even adults, which is why he tried to rent an attic room, also because there is less of a chance of anyone breaking in. Not that there's anything to steal, except a sewing machine, he adds.

"Next week I'll search for a job and a room," I say.

"There's enough room for both of us on the sofa," he says.

He looks past me.

"Besides, I'm not always home at night."

I sit on the bed and he reaches for the duffel bag, opens it and pulls out a brown suede coat.

"For you," he says with a smile. "It's the latest fashion in the British Isles."

He hands it to me.

"Try it on."

I stand up and slip on the coat. Meanwhile, he empties the bag and arranges more articles on the bed: a violet polo-neck sweater, a mini skirt, some kind of pinafore dress and a corduroy skirt. Finally he pulls out knee-high leather boots with heels and zippers on the side.

"You can't be spending all your wages on me," I say.

He says that when they docked, the second mate had sent him into town to buy food. On the way he'd been able to buy some clothes. While the crew went gallivanting around the harbour and got sloshed.

41

"I don't understand how you manage to get the foreign cash."

"I have connections. I know a cab driver who works up at the military base in Vellir.

"They've got currency."

I change clothes in the middle of the wooden floor and he doesn't look away. I first slip into the dress and leather boots and he tells me to walk up and down. I take two steps north and two steps south, two metres towards the harbour and two metres towards the graveyard.

"Hemlines are getting shorter," he says, and "should be five centimetres over the knee. And the skirt is supposed to be flared."

I take off the dress and slip into the skirt and parade back and forth. He observes me in silence and is clearly pleased.

Then I climb out of the skirt and put my trousers back on and sit on the bed beside Jón John.

"Next time I'll buy you a pantsuit with a belt."

I smile at him.

"They don't all come back, Hekla. Men go off on drinking binges and don't snap out of it and make it back to the boat before it sails off."

He hesitates.

"I considered vanishing and staying behind, but then I bought those boots and wanted to see you walking in them."

He stands up, walks over to the skylight and turns his back to me.

"I swear, Hekla, I won't always be here. In the back of beyond. I'm no match for the pounding surf. I'm going to leave. I want to see the world. Something more than Hull and Grimsby. I want to work in the theatre and make costumes for musicals. Or in fashion. There are more people like me abroad. A lot more."

I crucify the flesh by indulging it

I wake up as Jón John comes home just before dawn. He props himself up against the door, then the wall, falls into a chair, grabs the edge of the table and allows himself to slide onto the bed beside me in his clothes. I move over for him while he takes off his shoes. It takes a fairly long time for him to loosen his laces. He seems as if he hasn't slept, is drunk and reeks of aftershave.

I sit up and turn on the bedside lamp.

He looks battered, with dirt on his knees and scratches on his face. I see what I think are traces of gravel in his eyebrows, as if his face had been pressed into mud. I help him out of his clothes, fetch a damp towel and wash his face.

His eyes are open and watching me as I clean the grit out of his wounds.

"What happened?"

"Nothing."

"Where were you?"

"In the outskirts, the heathlands of Heidmörk," he says and lies down.

He curls up on the bed.

"I'm such a loser," I hear him say.

"Now now," I say.

After a short while, he adds: "There were two of them. I went to the Hábær bar and met a man who invited me for a drive. On the way he picked up a friend."

"We're going to the police."

"There's no point. Do you know what they do to perverts? I'm a criminal, a pathological freak. I'm hideous."

I spread the quilt over him.

"Besides, one of them is a cop and a prominent figure in the anti-homophile league."

He is quiet a moment and sniffs.

"They consider us the same as paedophiles. Mothers call in their children when a queer approaches. Queers' homes are broken into and completely trashed. They're spat on. If they have phones, they're called in the middle of the night with death threats."

He falls into such a long silence that I think he's fallen asleep.

"It's so difficult not to be scared," I hear him say under the quilt.

"You're the best man I know."

"I love children. I'm not a criminal."

I stroke his hair.

"Men only want to sleep with me when they're drunk, they don't want to talk afterwards and be friends. While they're pulling up their trousers, they make you swear three times that you won't tell anyone. They take you to the outskirts of Heidmörk and you're lucky if they drive you back into town."

He turns to the wall and I lie behind him and hold him. I envelop him against the wall like a child who must be protected from falling out of bed.

"Tomorrow I'll buy some iodine at the pharmacy," I say.

He grabs my hand. We huddle up tightly together, he's trembling.

"I wish I weren't the way I am, but I can't change that. Men are meant to go with women. I sleep with men."

He turns to face me.

"Did you know, Hekla, that just before the sun sinks into the ocean it gives off a green ray beyond the horizon?"

In the morning I rub the congealed mud from the knees of the trousers that Davíd Jón John Johnsson kicked off in the night.

With love from John

On my way to the pharmacy I buy a copy of the *Visir* newspaper and skim through the ads at the back. They're looking for a girl at the Fönn Laundry and at the bakery, and they also need a girl in the *Smørrebrød* open sandwich restaurant at Hotel Borg.

When I return, Jón John is lying on his stomach with his face buried in the sheets, his arms outstretched like a crucified man.

The *Passion Hymns* lie open beside him.

He doesn't want to talk about what happened last night.

"Are you okay?"

He turns around, sits up and combs back the hair on his forehead. One of his eyes is bloodshot.

"My head is full of black streams."

I put the bottle of iodine and plasters I bought at the pharmacy on the table and take off the suede coat.

"Thank you," he says without looking at me.

He stares at his hands, his open palms.

"I don't belong to any group, Hekla. I'm a mistake who shouldn't have been born."

He hesitates.

"I can't make sense of myself. I don't know where I come from. This earth doesn't belong to me. I only know what it's like to be pressed into it. I know how to chew gravel."

I sit beside him. He makes room for me.

"My mother met my father three times and slept with him once. A quick roll in the sack and that was it. The damage was done. She spent a year in Reykjavík answering the phone for Hreyfill taxis but never went to any parties

46

with the GIs. One day he showed up at the station. She said he had the hairstyle of some guy out of the movies, tidy and polite, with dark stubble, and that he smelt differently from Icelandic men. She sewed herself a light blue dress and he gave her a copy of Hemingway's *A Farewell to Arms* when he left and wrote in it: *With love from John.* Mom didn't understand English, but kept the book in the drawer of her bedside table.

"That was all she got from my father, his autograph and me. Then he was suddenly gone. The ship sailed off before he could say goodbye. She didn't know Dad's surname, just that he was called John and the army wouldn't help her. She didn't have any address for him. A friend of hers from Borgarnes, who'd also had a child with a soldier and who did have his address wrote him a letter. She got a postcard back with a picture of a graveyard that said: *Sorry about the baby, good luck and adieu.* At first she thought *adieu* meant see you again and it took her a long time to find out its true meaning. Mum felt it was likely that the ship had been sunk by a German torpedo. The bodies of soldiers sometimes washed up on the shores of Breidafjördur and she roamed the beaches to see if she would find the father of her child. She believed she would recognize John again, even if he was a washed-up corpse. She never fell in love again. There was no other man in her life.

"I was an illegitimate war child.

"Fatherless.

"'Your mum's a Yankee whore,' the kids used to say.

"'He wasn't actually a yank,' she told me long after-wards. 'Because your father was wearing a kilt when I met him. A chequered woollen kilt with a buckle. And nothing underneath.'"

The swan poet

"Read for me, Hekla."

"What do you want me to read?" I ask. "Shall I read some of Hallgrímur's psalms?"

I pick up the book lying open on the bed.

"Hallgrímur suffered like me," says my friend.

I glance at the spines on the bookshelf beside the bed.

I pull out some books and silently read the covers. Unlike the bookcases back home in Dalir, many of the books are in foreign languages. Apart from Lord Byron's biography, which is in Icelandic, there is a novel by Thomas Mann and a play by Oscar Wilde, *The Importance of Being Earnest*, but also poetry collections by Rimbaud, Verlaine and Walt Whitman. I notice that some of the books on the shelf are also by women: Virginia Woolf, Emily Dickinson and Selma Lagerlöf.

"That's my queer shelf," says Jón John from the bed.

He sits up, reaches for a book, opens it and skims through for a moment until he finds what he is looking for.

"If I die
Leave the balcony open

"He's my favourite poet, Federico García Lorca."

He hands me the book. *To Johnny boy* has been inscribed in a fountain pen on the first page. I put the book back on the shelf.

"From a friend at the military base in Vellir."

I tell him I want to learn English and that I'm reading a thick book by an Irish writer with the help of a dictionary, but that it's time-consuming and difficult.

"I'll ask my friend if he can give you lessons. You don't have to sleep with him," he adds. "I'll do that for you."

He hesitates.

"He'd be thrown out if he weren't an officer."

On the shelf there is a book by an Icelandic poet that seems at odds with the rest, *Black Feathers* by Davíd Stefánsson.

I pull it out.

"Mum waited a whole year to baptize me, in case a sea revenant stepped onto the shore. While she waited she read her favourite poet.

"She couldn't decide whether I should be called Davíd Stefánsson or Einar Benediktsson, it was a choice between *Black Feathers* and *Glimpse of the Ocean*.

"In the end she felt there were too many waves and too much pounding surf in Benediktsson. And too much of God in the surf, she said. My fate was therefore sealed with the sunrise poet who sang about the night that stores pleasure in its bosom, so I'm named after Iceland's swan poet and the unknown soldier who vanished into the billowy grey sea.

"Davíd Jón John Stefánsson Johnsson.

"The priest said the name was too long for the form and suggested Mum drop the Stefánsson.

"Otherwise people might think he's my illegitimate son, Revd Stefán is reported to have quipped. Impishly.

"She felt it would improve my prospects abroad too, if I were both Jón and John.

"'When you move abroad to find your roots, you will call yourself D.J. Johnsson,' she said to me."

He is silent for a long moment.

"Mum always knew I was different."

D.J. Johnsson stands up and totters over to the wardrobe. He opens it to pull out some black plumage that he drapes over his shoulders like a shawl. He looks like an eagle preparing to fly off the edge of a steep cliff.

"Mum kept a picture of the poet Davíd Stefánsson in her living room, holding a black raven in his arms. She cut it out of the newspaper and had it framed. I collected raven feathers and sewed myself a cape," he says.

"Come on," I say. "Let's go to Skálinn. I'll treat you to coffee and pancakes."

He puts the feathers back into the wardrobe and slips on a jacket.

"I don't fly the way you do, though, Hekla."

Homosexuals and existentialists

Two tramps are sitting on a bench in the cold sunshine, sipping methylated spirits from paper bags, by the southern wall of the Fisheries Bank. We sit at a window table and order coffee, Jón John has no appetite for pancakes. A group of poets are sitting at one of the tables inside the room, smoking pipes. One of them holds court, waving his hands in the air like the conductor of an orchestra; the other poets look at him and nod. I notice that one of the younger poets isn't participating in the conversation but is instead looking at me.

"I'm guessing they're either discussing rhymes or existentialism," says Jón John. There aren't many people about and I notice a middle-aged man in a dark coat and hat coming out of the bank with a briefcase, walking swiftly towards Austurstræti.

"That guy's queer," says Jón John, nodding towards the man. "He works at the bank. He's only into young boys and he's in a relationship with a bloke I know."

He sips his coffee and then rests his chin on one hand.

"Most of the men who hunt for boys like me are married family men and only queers at weekends. They get married to cover up their unnaturalness. Their wives know it. They know their husbands. Then many of the queers from around the country pretend they have a girlfriend and child back home in the countryside."

He looks down and buries his face in his hands.

"I don't want to be like them and live some secret game. I just want to love a guy like me. I want to hold his hand on the street. That'll never happen, Hekla."

"Have you met someone?"

"When I moved to Reykjavík, I was with a man for the first time. He wanted to know if I had any experience. I told him I had. I was afraid that he wouldn't want to be with me otherwise. He wasn't a lot older than I was, but he'd been with soldiers at the base in Vellir.

"He had this thing for uniforms."

The first time only happens once

"You were my first," I say.

He smiles.

"I know."

He lived in the village with his mother and I'd heard stories about him. That he knew how to use a sewing machine and had sewn kitchen curtains for his mother and put them up while she was at work. That he'd also made a Christmas dress for her. When I first met him, he was the shortest of the boys and I was the tallest of the girls. Then I went through puberty and stopped growing and he went through puberty and started to grow. He wore a bomber jacket like the one worn by James Dean in *Rebel Without a Cause*.*

It was said that he had made it from leftover pelts that had been given to him at the slaughterhouse, and that he'd managed to transform lamb skin into cow leather.

Like other youngsters, we worked in the slaughterhouse in the autumn, which is how our paths crossed, under the flayed carcasses of lambs that hung from hooks over the chlorine-washed stone floor. Initially, I was assigned to stirring the blood before it was canned and weighing the hearts, kidneys and livers, while he was in the freezer room, stacking soup meat in white gauze bags. One day I fetched him from a frosty white cloud of ice and we ate our picnics by the slaughterhouse wall in the limpid, cold autumn sunlight. The smell of congealed blood clung to us.

He was different from the other boys and didn't try to kiss me. It was then that I decided that he would be the first. Not that there were many candidates in the sparsely populated Dalir.

When the moment had come, I fetched a bottle of brandy that had been looted from a stranded ship and stored in the cabinet at home, untouched as far back as I can remember.

"Nobody will miss it," I said.

* James Dean's bomber jacket was sold at Palm Beach Modern Auctions in Florida in February 2018 for the price of $600,000.

We spent some time searching for a patch of geraniums or corrie where the grass hadn't been cut and was higher than our groins. Most important of all was that we were hidden from my brother, younger by two years, who tried to cling to us all the time. He was going to go to agricultural college and then take over the farm, 280 sheep and 17 cows, 14 of them red and 3 mottled. He had recently started to train in Icelandic wrestling and had become a member of the Dalir Young Men's Association. This now meant that he tried to wrestle any man who crossed his path. Even Revd Stefán was not exempt. My parents sometimes had to apologize to the guests my brother assaulted and invited to tackle him. They looked at him as if he were a stranger, unrelated to them, a teenager who followed his own laws but mainly his whims.

"He's training for the Grettir's Belt Cup," they would say hesitantly. My mother's expression seemed to express regret at having wasted an eagle's name on him. His first moves entailed clutching the guest's belt or grabbing his sleeve and twisting his garment in an effort to lift him up and knock him over with brute force, without losing his own balance. Gradually, his technique improved and he grew more agile and even demanded that his opponents be well versed in the wrestling jargon: upright position... step, step... trip and defend...

He was a slow developer and acned, listened to Cliff Richard, still pubescent and not yet in full control of his voice. The unwitting guests stepped back and forth and struggled in the ring.

"...Relax the arms... step... clockwise..." my brother could be heard saying.

After some time, we found the right spot, behind the sheep shed. Tall, green, whistling grass grew nearby. There we lay down, arms down by our sides, and gazed up at the sky, a wind-blown stratocumulus cloud. *I would rather have chosen a cumulus cloud or cloudless sky for my first time*, I wrote that evening. There were only five centimetres between us, which is the narrowest gap there can be between a woman and a man without touching. He was in a blue flannel shirt, I in a red skirt in honour of the day. We were both wearing waders.

"I wanted to touch the fabric of your skirt more than I wanted to touch what was underneath it," my friend now admits.

That was precisely what he did, asked me if he could touch the fabric. "Is that jersey?" he asked. He turned the hem, examined the lining, stroked it with his finger.

"Did you do the hemming yourself?" he asked.

"Are you afraid to touch me?" I said.

Then he first turned his attention to what was behind the fabric and his hand slid up towards the elastic of my panties. The moment had come to put my body on the line. To become a woman. I pulled up my skirt and he down his trousers.

Afterwards we sat side by side up on the hill and gazed at the shore of seaweed and islands in the fjord; his braces were down and he smoked. I spotted three seals on the shore.

Then I tell him.

That I write.

Every day.

That I started writing about the weather like my father and about the shades of light over the glacier beyond the fjord, that I described how white clouds lay like fleece over the glacier, and how people, events and places were then added.

"I feel like many things happen at once, like I see many images and experience many feelings at the same time, like I'm standing on some new starting point and it's the first day of the world and everything is new and pure," I say to my friend. "Like a spring morning in Dalir and I've just finished feeding the sheep in the barn and the bank of fog hovering over Breidafjördur lifts and dissolves. At that moment I'm holding the baton and tell the world it can be born."

In return the most handsome boy in Dalir told me that he loved boys.

We kept each other's secrets.

We were equals.

"People wondered why such a sweet boy didn't have a girlfriend. I knew I was queer. The only thing that could save me was to sleep with a girl. I'm glad it was you."

You've done it and I haven't

The next day I was quizzed about the bottle of brandy that had vanished from the cabinet in broad daylight and been returned after four big gulps.

My brother Örn conducts the interrogation. He is not satisfied.

He claims to be a witness to what he shouldn't have been a witness to.

"I saw you rush up the hill," he says. "And disappear behind it."

Now he follows me edgeways, trying to corner me, and bombards me with questions.

He wants to know where we went and what we were up to. Why he wasn't allowed to come? Whether Jón John had mentioned his name and, if so, what had he said, had he mentioned the wrestling? He continues to pressure me in the days that follow. Ultimately all the questions revolve around Jón John. Is he going away and, if so, where to? To Reykjavík? What's he going to do? Between the interrogations he sulks.

"Traitor," he ends up shrieking after me. Then I remember how he and Jón John were sparring once and, in some peculiar way, it reminded me more of birds dancing in a mating ritual than wrestling; it looked more like clumsy embraces than attacks. All of a sudden they were both lying on the grass. Then Jón John had broken free.

"Did you do it?" Ísey asks when I next see her.

"Yes."

"Then you've done it and I haven't," she says.

That meant that my best friend had to do it as well. In August a group of labourers came west to lay electrical cables and Ísey got pregnant, moved to Reykjavík and got married. Jón John went not long after her with the sewing machine and hoped to get a job in the National Theatre's wardrobe department or, as a backup, in the Vogue fabric store in Skólavördustígur.

"You saved my life, Hekla. When we became friends, people left me in peace. I thought to myself: she's like me."

Skyr

I have two job interviews today: one in a dairy shop that's also a bakery and another at Hotel Borg. I start with the dairy shop.

The middle-aged baker receives me in a quilted apron, standing on a black-and-white stone tiled floor with a drain in the middle. He treats me informally and shows me around the shop: what shelves the regular loaves of bread are stocked on, white bread here and rye bread there, how the glazed buns and Danish pastries should be arranged and how the pastry should be sliced.

"You get to keep the tag ends of the Danish pastries and

take them home," he says. Finally he makes me practise serving glazed buns over the counter.

"Imagine it's some high school boy," he says merrily.

In the end he fetches a tub of skyr from the fridge and wants me to practise wrapping a dollop of it in waxed paper.

He guides me.

"You fold the corners of the paper underneath," he says.

He says he would go home to rest when I arrive in the mornings and then come back in the afternoons to balance the cash register. But that I'd have to clean the store and tidy up. I stand on the stone floor as he stares at me.

"I could well imagine bun sales increasing with you behind the counter, those high school boys will be standing there with gaping jaws. With that waist and those hips."

He then wants to know where I live.

I tell him I'm living with a friend until I find a room.

"Is he your boyfriend?"

"No."

He ogles me.

"You could live at my place. I have a spare room in the cellar."

Serving girl wanted at Hotel Borg

The other option was the serving girl job at Hotel Borg. I wait for the man I'm supposed to meet at the bar. The counter is dark wood and the bartender leans over to me, knocks on the timber and says:

"Palisander."

Jón John has told me that gays seek each other out at the bar here on weekends. And that he sometimes watches how a man dances with a woman in the Gilded Ballroom.

While I'm waiting I contemplate a giant painting of Mt Esja and the islands in the bay between the mountain and the city. A fishing boat floats on the strait and in the foreground one can make out seagulls and puffins with colourful beaks, on the shore as the sun sinks into the sea.

The man ushers me into the office where he jots down some notes about me.

"So you're from Dalir?"

He eyes me up.

"We don't hide our beauty queens in the kitchen, instead we'll put you out serving in the dining room."

He stands.

"You're hired and start on Monday at nine. And one other thing, Miss Hekla, you won't serve in trousers, but in a skirt. You'll get your uniform on Monday."

The head waiter escorts me through the smoking corner of the dining room, between the starched white tablecloths. There are silver sugar bowls and cream jugs on the tables and crystal chandeliers in the air. He gives me a briefing, speaking in hushed tones, and tells me that the bulk of the customers are a group of elderly gentlemen, who are considered permanent guests and show up for the cold buffet at noon, when it's jam-packed, and elderly ladies who come in for coffee and cakes in the mid-afternoon, usually in twos or threes. The bar is open for two hours during the day, from eleven to one, which is when the select clientele gets drunk; many of them become unruly and difficult to handle. Then there are the high school boys who come in and order coffee with sugar cubes and nothing else, and sit here for ages smoking, he explains. They're bunking off school, have poetry books in their pockets and dream of becoming poets. Once they've had a poem published in the school mag they move over to Skálinn, Mokka or Laugavegur 11, he concludes.

I notice a woman in a black skirt and white apron and cap atop a dome-shaped structure of lacquered hair, who is standing with a coffee pot by a round table, pouring into the cups of a group of middle-aged men. She observes me.

"There will be two of you in the dining room with the waiters," he explains.

Finally he shows me the Gilded Ballroom where Ellý Vilhjálms sings with Jón Páll's band on weekends, as well as the back rooms and dressing rooms, adding that there are forty-six bedrooms in the hotel that can accommodate seventy-three guests. Next week Lyndon B. Johnson, the vice-president of the United States, is expected in the country and, even though Johnson himself will be staying at the newly opened Hotel Saga, a part of his entourage will be staying at Hotel Borg. He lowers his voice even further to inform me that the vice-president is interested in vegetation and livestock, and has expressed some interest in visiting Icelandic farmlands. As he says this, he indicates someone with a nod of the chin:

"That's one of the heads of the Sheep Farmers' Association sitting over at the corner table with the director of the Reykjavík Sewage System. It seems likely that Mrs Johnson will be visiting his sheep farm." To complete the tour, he shows me how to clock in and out with my card.

When we walk through the kitchen, the woman who was serving in the dining room is standing by the sink, smoking. She fans the smoke away, stubs out the cigarette, chucks it in the bin, grabs a tray with prawn mayonnaise open sandwiches and prepares to swing back into the room.

"Sirrí, this is Hekla. The new serving girl. She'll be working in the dining room with you."

I stretch out my hand and she nods without putting down the tray.

I work it out in my head: If I work nine hours and sleep for seven, I'll have eight hours left over in the day to write and read. If I want to write at night, there's no one to stop me. And no one who is encouraging me to do so either. No one is waiting for a novel by Hekla Gottskálksdóttir.

The man in the Snæbjörn bookstore allows me to put an ad up in the window.

Single girl with full-time job looking for room to rent. Punctual monthly payments.

I have a dream

The sofa is covered in newspaper cuttings.

I bend over and swiftly skim through them. They're in both Icelandic and English and they all seem to be about the black American pastor Martin Luther King.

"The black rights campaigner," says Jón John. "I've been collecting these. The blacks aren't free, no more than we are. But they've recently found a voice."

He bends to smooth out some of the crumpled cuttings with his hands, reads in silence and carefully rearranges them on the sofa.

His lips are moving.

"*I dream of a world in which there is a place for everyone,*" he says.

I notice the Icelandic cuttings are shorter than the others, by just a few lines. My friend confirms this.

"King gave his speech at the March on Washington for Jobs and Freedom last month, but none of the Icelandic papers reports what he said." He picks up a few clips:

"*Althydubladid* on August the 29th mentions the march and that the black leader gave a speech but doesn't quote any of it. *Morgunbladid* makes very little of the march and doesn't say a single word about Martin Luther King or the speech. But it says that some famous artists participated in the march to draw the limelight to themselves. It also says that there were fewer people than expected. But it was still a higher number than the entire Icelandic population put together, Hekla."

He takes a deep breath.

"But since Icelanders have no interest in Martin Luther King," he continues, "his friend down south at the Vellir base has procured him some American papers that his sister sent him from back home." Jón John browses through the collection searching for a particular clipping, pulls out the article and translates for me as he reads:

"I have a dream that my four little children will one day live in a nation where they will not be judged by the colour of their skin but by the content of their character... I have a dream today!"

He has tears in his eyes.

"King says the black man's problems are the white man's problems." He carefully puts the cutting back in its place and looks me in the eye.

"The problems of gays are the problems of non-gays, Hekla."

He folds the paper cuttings, one after another, collects them together and puts them back in their place in the Sælgætisgerdin Nóa sweets tin, opens the wardrobe and places the box at the bottom of it beside the sewing machine.

He shakes his head.

"I've tried in vain to get a job at the Vellir base, but they don't want any blacks or queers. Even though I'm half soldier. Queers get kicked out of the army and jailed if they're found out. They're looked upon as child molesters and communists." He sits down on the bed beside me.

"The Icelandic government negotiated a deal to make sure there would be no blacks at the base. They sent one over by mistake last year, and they let him stay on condition that he never left the barracks. He had a tough time this summer because he couldn't sleep in the sunlight at night."

He's silent for a brief moment and then says:

"My blood runs in the veins of so many, Hekla. Both in those who've gone and those who have yet to be born."

He then wants to know how the job interviews went. I tell him I've been given a job as a serving girl in Hotel Borg.

"I'm supposed to serve in a skirt and not in trousers."

He smiles.

I also tell him that his namesake, Johnson, the vice-president of the United States, is coming to the country next week.

"Might he be a distant relative?" I add. "L.B. Johnson and D.J. Johnson?"

"There's a difference of one 's'. I'm Johnsson with two s's. The son of John."

The Beauty Society

The trays are heavy, once they have been loaded with coffee pots, silver sugar bowls and cream jugs.

The head waiter is keeping an eye on me on my first day at the job. So is my colleague Sirrí.

"This is my serving area and that's yours," she says. "You serve those tables and I serve these tables." She watches and is waiting for me when I come back into the kitchen after my first trip with the tray. She wants to warn me that certain punters can get difficult when they've had a few drinks.

"The older men are the worst," she says.

"If they pinch you, then come into the kitchen and we'll switch tables. They grab you when you walk past. They grope your arse and run a hand up your skirt. They'll also fondle your breasts when you're pouring into their cups. Then they'll do everything to make us bend over. Normally they'll drop a teaspoon. Once a waiter wanted to spare me the trouble and was about to bend over for the spoon, but the customer insisted on me doing it. They whisper into your ear, follow you, want to know where you live. They wait for the serving girls after they've finished their shifts. One drunken regular customer followed a girl into the larder when she was getting some mayonnaise. He cornered her there and tried to touch her up like a piece of meat. If they follow you out onto the street, go into the lingerie store at the bottom of Skólavördustígur and ask them to let you use the back door out of the storage room. They won't dare follow you in there." She mentions some other stores that have a backdoor exit such as the Liverpool domestic appliances store. I feel like asking her whether there are any bookstores that save damsels in distress, whether it's possible to hide there, even for a whole night, alone with a book, but I refrain.

"Beginners face the highest risk," she adds.

"If you complain they'll say: that's the way it's always been, get used to it.

"One girl lost her balance when she was pinched and dropped her tray. She was a single mother and had a kid to look after. She got a warning and was transferred to cleaning the rooms. That's said to be even worse because the chambermaids are alone with guests who walk around naked in open dressing gowns while they're vacuum-cleaning. I don't know what happened, but one day she came down from the third floor, crying and was in a real state. They took her into the office."

My colleague blows her smoke into concentric rings and then stubs out the cigarette.

"They said she wasn't the right type for this kind of job."

When I walk back into the room to collect the dirty crockery, I notice a familiar man sitting at a round table with a group of old men, watching me.

He's had the meat soup and is carefully cleaning the meat off the bones and sucking out the marrow. A pile of bones lies on the rim of the plate.

He addresses me through a cloud of cigar smoke.

"So you've started waitressing at Hotel Borg."

I look up, it's the man from the coach, the one from the Beauty Society who gave me his business card.

"Do you enjoy laying tables?"

He doesn't wait for an answer but continues.

"I only ask because one of the tests in the Miss Iceland competition entails precisely that: laying a table and folding serviettes."

He adds that the competition is still being developed and they are also considering asking the girls to have a go at repotting plants.

"Are you interested in house plants?"

"No."

"Needlework?"

"No."

"Reading good books?"

"No, only bad books."

He looks at me uncertainly and laughs.

"So the girl has a sense of humour."

The man leans over to his neighbour and mutters something, as if he were putting him into the picture. His table companion eyes me up and nods his head.

Then he turns to me again and asks if I've thought the matter over.

"What matter?"

"Can I invite you to become Miss Iceland?"

"No, thank you."

The man continues unabated.

"You'll get to travel abroad, a limousine and private chauffeur."

I quickly pick up the dishes.

"...Miss Iceland gets a crown and sceptre, a blue Icelandic festival costume with a golden belt for the competition on Long Island, two gowns and a coat with a fur collar. She gets to stand onstage and go to nightclubs and meet famous boxers and she gets her picture in the papers."

As I hurry away, I hear the man say:

"You should raise your skirt above the knees. It's a shame to hide such beautiful knees. It's important to doll yourself up."

Sirrí is waiting for me behind the swinging doors in the kitchen and with a tip of the chin, indicates a man at the round table I need to watch out for.

"Several girls have been pestered by him."

When I've hung up my apron and punched out, my colleague comes rushing after me. She tells me she knows a girl who participated in Miss Iceland a few years back when the competition was still held in the open air in Vatnsmýri and now works at the switchboard at the Hreyfill cab company. She can introduce me to her if I want.

"She was also promised a fur coat and trips abroad. It never happened."

"I'm not thinking of participating," I say.

She adjusts her headscarf around her hair, lights a cigarette and puffs smoke out of the corner of her mouth.

"I just wanted you to know."

The ocean planets

Jón John has given up trying to find a job on land.

"It's hopeless," he says. "I'm going to have to take another fishing trip. Even if it kills me. Even if I sink with the rusty wreck. I'm named after the swan poet, not after the sea poet, I'm not *the son of rocks and waves*."

He is lying on the bed and says he's thinking of heading west to the fjords, where he can get a place on the Freyja motorboat from Tálknafjördur or a temporary herring-fishing job with the boat *Trausti* in Ísafjördur. Is it more trustworthy to choose a boat that is named after a man or a woman? He's also considering spending the winter in a fishing factory in Neskaupsstadur in the east. But wages are low everywhere and people are brazenly cheated.

"It'll take me a year to save enough to go abroad," he adds.

He stands up, walks up to the skylight and stands there, staring into the darkness.

"A last resort would be to get hired on that rusty trawler raft again, *Saturnus*, emptying the net.

"I could try choosing one of the other ocean planets: maybe Pluto, Neptune or Uranus?"

I walk over to my friend and place a hand on his shoulder.

"Not that it matters what planet or drunkards I go down to a watery grave with."

"Isn't it pretty dangerous to stand under those tons of fish?" I ask.

He paces the length of the floor.

"Unless I take a three-month salt-fish trip to Greenland. If the skipper isn't too drunk, there's a chance I'll survive the icebergs and polar bears."

By evening Jón John has decided to go to the western fjords, but by the following morning, he has changed his mind and been taken on by the *Saturnus* side trawler again, in the faint hope that he'll get to substitute for the cook, be left in peace and survive the trip.

"We sail tonight," he says, when I come home from work.

The duffel bag is ready by the bedroom door.

"We're sailing to Hull with the catch."

My friend dawdles in the middle of the floor and I can see there is something troubling him.

"I want to ask you to do me a favour, Hekla." He looks down at the splintered wooden floor and then past me before he continues, as if he were standing peering at the horizon in the offing, and not under a barely habitable dormer bedroom on Stýrimannastígur.

"I wanted to ask you to see me off at the docks."

He hesitates.

71

"I told them the clothes were for my girlfriend, but they wouldn't believe me and wanted to see you."

I've never drowned myself

Splinters of white scatter in the air and the wind is picking up, so I button up my suede coat and put on some gloves. My sailor, on the other hand, is bareheaded in a wool sweater. Darkness has fallen and the warehouses by the harbour are closed. Between the slippery wooden planks, one can glimpse the oil-patched sea. The rusty trawler stands at the end of the wharf.

The crew is boarding, staggering on their feet, with hands in their pockets and cigarettes in their mouths. Some come straight from the pubs in crumpled suits and Sunday best shoes. I can't help staring at two who are heading up the gangway, both wearing ties and patent leather shoes. One of them is holding the other under the arm, actually dragging him along, while the other has a bottle from which he occasionally sips. When he spots Jón John, he tries to wave the bottle in our direction, but trips and slips on the gangway.

"There's the fucking freak with a lady on his arm," I hear him say. Once he's regained his balance with some difficulty, like a newborn foal trying to stand on its legs for the first time, he runs a comb through his brilliantined hair and, after several attempts, manages to fish a cigarette out of a packet in his pocket and light it.

"Aren't you going to invite the lady down to the cabin?" the other calls out, slurring.

"That's Konni Nonsense and Steini Nozzle," says Jón John. "Coming straight from the Rödull club."

He smiles faintly.

"They have nicknames like poets," he adds.

I grab my friend's hand, he looks at me with gratitude and holds on to it tightly like a drowning man to a life buoy.

"I'll buy some books for you in Hull," he says.

I escort him to the gangway and embrace him, waves lapping under our feet.

"You're not allowed to drown," I say.

"It's not the worst thing that can happen. It doesn't take long to croak in the cold."

I hug him tight.

"I won't, out of consideration for Mum," he adds. A seagull draws a circle in the air, for a moment the bird hovers straight above us and allows its legs to sink as if it were preparing to land, but then with two flaps of the wings the bird vanishes into the white shaft of hail over *Saturnus*.

Medea

I hand Ísey a white waxed box containing four canapés. It took some effort to wrestle it all the way over to Nordurmýri in the stormy weather. I notice she has moved the cot out of the bedroom into the living room.

"That way I can keep an eye on Thorgerdur during the day," she says. "She sleeps in my bed at night."

She lays her daughter down in the cot, lifts up the lid of the box and smiles from ear to ear. I see that the canapés have shifted in transit and that streaks of mayonnaise have been smudged and squashed with the prawns. She puts them in the fridge and then sits facing me at the kitchen table. The door to the living room is open and she keeps an eye on the child.

"Remember I told you I had started to write a journal? Which isn't exactly a journal, though."

"Yes, I remember that."

"I walked all the way into town with the pram yesterday and bought another journal. Battling the storm. The man in Gudgeir's stationery store remembered me well. He advised me to buy copybooks instead or squared exercise books since I was so quick to fill them up and it would be cheaper. They're the only treat I allow myself." She is quiet for a moment as she prepares coffee.

"I've started to write conversations," she finally says.

"What kind of conversations? Things people say?"

"Both what people say and what they don't say. I can't explain it to Lýdur: that when he says something, I want to write it down. And even less that I write down the things he doesn't say. Nor would he understand that I sometimes want to stop what I'm doing and write about it instead."

My friend's head droops.

"The other day we were invited to my parents-in-law in Efstasund and my sisters-in-law were there as well. They get the Yankee TV channel from the military base, which is really difficult to get. One line Dröfn came out with about her husband made me excuse myself and escape into another room to write down a few sentences."

She shakes her head.

"Imagine, Hekla, I've started to walk around with a notepad in my handbag."

She pours coffee into my cup and then adjusts the clip in her hair.

"When we got home and Lýdur had fallen asleep, I continued writing conversations. Before I knew it, I'd written eighteen pages about a woman who discovers her husband is having an affair and takes revenge by murdering their child. Lýdur wouldn't understand that."

She lifts the child out of the cot and places her on her hip.

"Tell me what's happening out there, Hekla, tell me who comes to Hotel Borg, tell me about life beyond Kjartansgata."

Should I tell her about all the men who won't stop pestering me, who leer at me and seize every opportunity to touch me without my permission? Who ask me out. Powerful men. I always politely decline. They don't take it well. They're used to having their own way and getting the girls who spurn them fired. Instead I tell my friend who writes conversations at night that I've now got a municipal library card from Thingholtsstræti and can take out books for her.

Ísey wants us to move into the living room. She hands me the child, gets the cups and places them on the coffee table.

I notice that yet another Kjarval painting has been added to the collection because there are now three. To fit them in she's had to move the sideboard and hang one painting above the other so that the brown frame of one of them almost touches the ceiling. Ísey says that they now have landscapes from three different parts of the country in their tiny living room.

She drops into the sofa and assumes a grave air. It transpires she's dreamt a dream.

"I dreamt," she says, "that we had moved into a new house and all of the furniture was made out of palisander wood and there was a long staircase up to the top floor, lots of steps, and I held Thorgerdur in my arms. There were four children's bedrooms in the house. Now I'm scared that means I'll have four children."

Odin
(or when I acquired the God of poetry and wisdom)

Dusk is starting to fall and at the bottom of Ódinsgata I hear a piteous cry coming from the top of a tree that stands beside a green corrugated-iron house. It's the only tree on the street. I look up and make out a scrawny creature hanging on a branch and feebly meowing. I find my footing in a cleft at the bottom of the trunk, climb up the tree, manage to grab the terrified animal and lower it down to the pavement. The cat isn't fully grown, black but for a white spot over a missing eye and untagged. I stroke it a few times, but then have to hurry home because I want to finish a chapter. When I get down to Austurstræti, the animal is still behind me and follows me all the way up to Stýrimannastígur. I open the hall door and the cat immediately shoots past me and up the steep wooden stairs, where it waits on the narrow landing and meows. I let it in.

I pour milk into a bowl.

I've acquired a cat.

I stroke it several times.

A cat owns me.

The following morning a raven perches on a lamp post outside the skylight and croaks. The kids throw stones at it and when it launches into flight, I notice that one of its wings is damaged.

The joy of being alive and knowing that I'm going home to write

I clock out at five.

I walk past Snæbjörn and Bragi Brynjólfsson's bookstore windows in Hafnarstræti every day and often go in to browse through their shelves. I've already decided which books I'm going to buy when I get paid. In Hafnarstræti there's also the Nordra Bookstore, which sells the *Nordisk Konversations leksikon* encyclopaedia in eight volumes through monthly instalments, bound in leather with gold-embossed letters. In Austurstræti there's the Ísafold bookshop and in Bankastræti there is Kron's; on Laugavegur there are the Mál og menning, Bókhladan and Helgafell bookstores. Lárus Blöndal's bookstore is on Skólavördustígur. That's my circuit. I've also walked all the way to the new park at Klambratún and back, and looked at the trees that have recently been planted there.

I get paid on Friday. Then I'll go to Landsbankinn on Austurstræti and pay it into my account. In the bank there are murals by the same artist who did the paintings that Ísey's father-in-law wanted to get rid of. They depict women stacking salt fish. My wages are lower than I'd expected. Sirrí informs me that serving girls get half what waiters get.

"Even though we split the room in two and serve as many tables as they do. That's how it's always been and that's how it will always be, they say. I just wanted you to know that," she adds.

Occasionally I buy myself a coffee at Skálinn, but when I get canapés for Ísey they're deducted from my wages. I've walked out to Grótta twice, all the way to the lighthouse, and stood there in the slippery seaweed, listening to the hiss of the surf until it faded. Sea foam whirls high in the wind.

Somewhere on the other side of the strait and the headland topped by the glacier that contains the exact centre of the earth, Dad sits writing his descriptions of the weather. Even further out in the white surfy ocean is the seasick Jón John on his way to Hull with fish in the hold. While I'm serving in the Hotel Borg, I keep the story alive in my mind. Even though I'm in the middle of pouring coffee, my mind isn't there; I'm elsewhere, because I'm thinking about what I'm going to write in the evening when I've clocked out.

"Miss," says a woman, "there are no sugar cubes."

Occasionally I scribble a few words on a napkin and stick it in my pocket when I collect an order from the kitchen.

"Are you writing down a phone number?" Sirrí asks.

The man from the Beauty Society shows up for the lunchtime buffet every day and sometimes comes in the afternoon and has a coffee with sugar and a slice of cream cake. Sirrí offered to switch areas with me so that I wouldn't have to serve him. But he still waved at me from the other side of the room.

"Another pot of coffee, miss."

When I bend over to place the pot on the white table-cloth, he says:

"I'll be your personal tour guide in Long Island. Surely you're not going to squander the rest of your life as a waitress?"

When I'm hanging up my apron one day, the head waiter comes up with a big square white box which he hands to me.

"With compliments from the round table," he says and smiles.

I lift the lid. The box contains a tart with pink marzipan shaped like a woman in a long dress. She has a red maraschino cherry on each breast and ornate lettering in chocolate icing:

Miss Volcano

Sirrí glances at the tart.

"I just want you to know, Hekla," she says, "that you dared to do things that other waitresses would have been fired for. Like telling that guy sitting with the director of the sewage company that enough was enough and, when he refused to back off, having the guts to pour coffee over the sleeve of his jacket. And then apologizing with a smile. And for that you get a marzipan tart."

Poets are entrusted with the care of books

When I'm not writing, I go to the municipal library in Thingholtsstræti where I'm a member. The fee is five krónur a year and members can take out three books at a time. The building is surrounded by trees and has a high ceiling with ornate plasterwork in the corners and a fluffy carpet on the floor. I sometimes dash over there during my breaks and manage to read a collection of poems. The head librarian is an old poet who wrote a beautiful poem about the desert.

Also working at the municipal library in Thingholtsstræti is a young librarian I had spotted a few times at Skálinn hanging out with the poets. I've caught him observing me when I'm standing at a bookshelf browsing through a book.

When I lay Thomas Mann's *The Magic Mountain* on his counter, he smiles at me and says: "Life, death, love."

He's wearing a white shirt with a tie under a knitted sweater. I also put down two poetry books I'm going to take to Ísey.

"It's mainly the poetry books that people are reluctant to return," he says. "They love those the most. We've even had to collect poetry books from people's homes."

He then stands up and offers to take me on a tour of the library. He says they store manuscripts from the Icelandic Society for the Advancement of Learning and have also stocked *Skírnir* magazine since its first issue in 1827, but that the library's real treasure is a precious beautifully bound copy of the *Fjölnir* journal. The librarian guides me between the rows of books and says they have an important collection of travel literature by foreigners who have explored Iceland, such as, for example, the botanist Hooks who toured the country with Jørgen the Dog-Days King, as well as a book by Lord Dillon and the story of John Barrow's journey from 1834.

"I couldn't help noticing how you handle the books," he continues. "You pick one up, open it, read the beginning, browse through it and then read a few more lines. Then you skim rapidly through it until you come to the last page, there you pause and read the ending. And put the book back on the shelf. Then you pick up the next book and follow the same method. It's very unusual for people to read books in the order they're shelved."

A swinging door

The next day the librarian is sitting at a corner table at Hotel Borg.

He's alone, holds a book in his hand, smokes a pipe and watches me. He orders a fourth cup of coffee and smiles at me every time I hand him a new cup. I notice he's reading Sveinbjörn Egilsson's translation of the *Odyssey*. There is also a notebook with a black cover and a fountain pen beside him on the table. I observe how he occasionally opens it, uncaps the pen and scribbles a note.

I look the owner of the Mont Blanc in the eye.

"Starkadur," he says assertively, thrusting out his hand.

I can't resist.

"Are you writing?"

He nods and says he works at the library for half the day, but that otherwise he writes poetry and has been working on a short story. It transpires that he's had one poem published in the *Eimreid* magazine.

The head waiter has appeared; he takes me by the shoulder and ushers me away from the table.

"The ladies by the window are out of sugar cubes, Miss Hekla."

When I return to the kitchen, he is waiting for me.

"Waitresses aren't supposed to fraternize with customers. I can see perfectly well what's going on."

"What's going on?"

"Flirtation. We all know what that leads to. Girls get pregnant and quit."

"He's a poet," I say.

"Poets get girls pregnant too."

He holds the swinging door into the room open with one hand and tips his head in the direction of a man sitting by the window.

"Instead of falling for a penniless poet you could catch a better suitor. There are loads of single men who need a woman to brighten up their lives. There by the window, for example, is a newly qualified and unattached engineer who owns an apartment in Sóleyjargata and a second-hand Ford."

Guardian woman

The librarian stays put until I've finished my shift, then springs to his feet and asks if he can walk with me. We first walk over to Lækjartorg, where a cold wind blows in from the sea, then we wander aimlessly south of the Lake towards Skothúsvegur. On the way, he tells me that there are books by 706 Icelandic authors in the library, a total of 71,719 books.

He wants me to guess which genre is the most popular among members.

"Poetry books?" I ask.

The poet laughs.

"Novels."

He explains that women read novels and since they make up the majority of members, novels are the books that are lent out the most. Books on historical subjects and national issues are the most popular among men, on the other hand. The third most popular category of books are those about distant countries.

"Both men and women are curious to know about what things are like abroad," he says, winding up his report.

I ask him which novels are taken out the most.

He ponders a moment.

"That would probably be children's books by Ragnheidur Jónsdóttir and the rural novels of Gudrún frá Lundi," he says with some reluctance.

"Books by two women," I say.

He hesitates.

"Yes, that's true actually, now that you mention it. Which is pretty weird considering there are so few female novelists in Iceland and they're all bad."

The topic of the library has been exhausted, but once we've walked over to Tjarnargata, the librarian halts by a corrugated-iron building and says that this is the headquarters of the Icelandic socialists and that he attends meetings there. The Youth Movement. A placard in the window reads *Fight against capitalism*.

Suddenly we're in the graveyard along Sudurgata. The lychgate creaks. The earth is a decaying swamp, there is death at every step. Nature is an open grave.

"This is where the poets rest," says my guide. "Even the immortal ones."

"Yes, I say, the dead all look alike."

The librarian glances at me and is on the point of saying something but stops, and instead waltzes between the tombstones looking for various resting places. Despite having the rhymes and poetic quotations of both Benedikt Gröndal and Steingrímur Thorsteinsson at his fingertips, he can't find his way to them; the poets won't give themselves away.

"They should be here somewhere," he says, unable to conceal his disappointment. "They were here the other day when I came here with Dadi Dream-fjörd."

The dark autumn evening seeps out of the earth and I'm cold. Wet, yellowing grass brushes against my ankles. I think of Mum.

"Isn't the novelist Theodóra Thoroddsen buried here?" I ask.

The librarian is distracted and by no means certain, but says he fully expects she is resting with her husband Skúli. Darting between the tombstones and skimming through the epitaphs, he is unable to contain his joy when he stumbles on Thorsteinn Erlingsson. He calls me over and fervently breaks into "The Snow Bunting":

> *"Her voice was so fair and so warm and so pure*
> *Warbling to me from this tiny wee bush…*
> *and night after night she chanted love poems alone…"*

In the middle of the cemetery is a tombstone belonging to a woman who died in 1838 and strikes me because of the length of its inscription:

> *…was the mother of five children who died at a young age, as strong as two giants, a protector of the poor, caring mother, sincere, good hearted…*

"She's the guardian of this cemetery, the first to be buried here," says my guide, sidling up to me. He looks at me and I can sense there is something weighing on him:

"Actually I was going to invite you to the pictures this evening," he says. "I've been manning myself up," he adds.

"They're showing a Fellini movie in the Austurbær Cinema, *Cleopatra* in the New Cinema, *Two Women* with Sophia Loren in the Old Cinema and *Lawrence of Arabia* in Tónabíó," he rattles off.

"I want to see *To Kill a Mockingbird* which they're screening in Stjörnubíó at nine," I say.

I'd seen the book on display in the window of the Snæbjörn Bookstore in Hafnarstræti.

"The book is by a woman," I say. "Harper Lee."

I surprise him.

He looks at me in wonderment.

"You're the most bookish waitress I've ever met."

That's the truth. Not necessarily the reality

We meet outside the cinema at a quarter to nine and he waves the tickets at me. We sink into deep burgundy-leather seats with silver-studded armrests. We're sitting in the middle of the theatre, the smoky shimmering beam of the projector glowing above us. I try to listen to the language as I read the subtitles on the screen, but it's difficult. Farming work in America's Deep South is also quite different from what we're used to in Dalir. In the middle of the movie, the poet slips an arm around my shoulder.

"I would have expected a woman to choose a different movie," he says when we walk out.

When I say: "The blacks still aren't liberated, no more than gays are," he looks at me as if he were struggling to respond. It's difficult to fathom what's going through his head. He has beautiful hands and I'm willing to sleep with him if he asks me to.

Suddenly we're up on Skólavördustígur where the poet rents a room. A few drunken couples stagger past us here and there, but there are no cars on the road.

"The Mokka café is just a few yards down there," he says and smiles.

I feel my heart pounding.

He tells me that the room he rents is under a sloping ceiling and that the square metres under the window aren't actually calculated into the rent. I have to make a quick decision: am I going to go home and write or sleep with the poet?

Certain situations can only be dealt with by removing one's clothes. I'm not wearing fancy underwear but he doesn't care, he just wants me out of it as quickly as possible.

Afterwards the poet slips some Shostakovich onto the record player and I glance around the room and the ceiling, which is barely high enough for a grown man, except in the centre.

I mull over when might be the right time to leave and what is the right amount of time to stay.

The poet tells me he's from Hveragerdi, where his mother lives, and that his father had been a deckhand on the *Dettifoss* until the boat was struck by a German torpedo in the war and sank.

"I was four years old and my sisters two and six when he died," he says.

In return I tell him that I'm temporarily living with a male friend while he's out at sea.

"He's like a brother to me," I add.

I'm about to say: He's my best friend, but stop myself.

By the bed there is a cabinet containing three shelves of books behind a glass door. Unable to resist, I scan the spines. It's like Dad's book cabinet. There's *Njál's Saga* and *Grettir's Saga*, *Sturlunga*, *Heimskringla* and *Snorri's Edda*, and *Wakeful Nights* by Stephan G. Stephansson. One shelf is devoted to anthologies by the national poets with the works of Jónas Hallgrímsson, Steingrímur Thorsteinsson and Hannes Hafsteinn. There are also novels by Laxness, Gunnar Gunnarsson and Thorberg Thordarson, Jón á Bægisá's translation of Milton's *Paradise Lost* and two translated books, *Hunger* by Hamsun and *The Odyssey*. All the books are leatherbound.

"*Laxdæla* is missing," I say.

The poet raises himself on his elbows.

"Yes, that's right," he says after some thinking, "you're from Dalir."

He stretches his arm over to me.

I could leave now and write for an hour before I go to work.

Or not.

When I get home, the cat is waiting for me in front of the hall door.

I bend over and stroke it.

The remains of a bird lie scattered on the pavement: a beak, one wing and two feathers.

I need to be alone. Many. Alone

My friend is pensive and seems anxious.

"My life is over, Hekla."

"What happened?"

"Imagine, a bag of blood burst when we were making blood pudding at my sisters-in-law, Lýdur's sisters, and splashed all over me. The strange thing is I started to cry. My sisters-in-law stared at me and I felt so ashamed. Hrönn asked me if I was pregnant."

"And are you? Are you expecting another baby?"

She averts her gaze.

"You must be thinking what have I gotten myself into? Don't you think it's awful? I think it's awful. I'm so happy. I've no appetite. I was really looking forward to getting some freshly boiled blood pudding, but I can't keep anything down. It wasn't planned, but it'll be good for Thorgerdur to get a playing companion. Lýdur is happy. He feels one child isn't a family. A family is nothing less than three children, he says. I haven't told him I think two is enough."

I stand up and embrace my friend.

She's as thin as a rake. I can feel her ribs.

"Congratulations."

I think: It's growing in the darkness.

"I knew you'd take it like that. Wonder what I got myself into. I really dreaded telling you."

I hold her tight.

"It'll work out."

"It's still almost invisible. Then it will grow and need to be born.

"Thorgerdur was four kilos. I'll die, Hekla. I didn't realize giving birth was so painful. I was in labour for two days and I had so many stitches I couldn't sit for three weeks."

"It'll be fine."

She wipes her eyes.

"I'm named after an iceberg. Pack ice flowed into Breidafjördur the spring I was born. Dad wanted to add an island to the fjord and baptized me *Ísey*, Ice Island."

She is silent for a moment. Thorgerdur stands in the cot, and holds out her arms, wanting to be lifted. I pick up the child, she needs a change of nappy.

"It was so boxed in back home, the mountain lay on the other side of the field fence, I wanted to go away. I fell in love. I got pregnant. Next summer I'll be alone with two small children in a basement in Nordurmýri. Twenty-two years old."

My friend allows herself to drop onto the sofa, but then springs straight up again and says she's going to make some coffee. I change the girl's nappy in the meantime.

"Sorry, Hekla, I don't ask anything about you," she says when she returns with the coffee pot. "Have you met someone?"

"Yes, as a matter of fact."

She scrutinizes me.

"Who?"

"A librarian from the library in Thingholtsstræti. He's a writer as well," I add.

"Like you?"

"He doesn't know I write."

"Haven't you told him you've been published?"

"That was under a pseudonym."

It had actually been Ísey who had come up with the idea that I take on a poet's name, the way male poets do. "Preferably something fancy like Hekla Zenith," she suggested.

"No," I said, laughing.

She wouldn't give in.

"Isn't there some dale, some stream, some spot that you can name yourself after? If you want to go for something fancy we need to delve deeper, how about Deep Canyon...?"

"No."

"That was tongue in cheek by the way," she now says.

She studies me.

"Didn't you tell the poet you were writing a novel either?"

"No."

"And have completed two manuscripts?"

"I haven't had an answer from the publisher."

"What do you do together?"

"We sleep together."

I'm relieved she hasn't asked whether I prefer to write or sleep with him, which is the most important: the bed or the Remington typewriter?

That's her next question.

"Which do you want the most, to have a boyfriend or write books?"

I give it some thought. In my dream world the most important things would be: a sheet of paper, fountain pen and a male body. When we've finished making love, he's welcome to ask if he can refill the fountain pen with ink for me.

She has a serious air and gazes beyond me.

"Women have to choose, Hekla."

"Both in equal measure," I answer. "I need to be both alone and not alone," I add.

"That means that you are both a writer and ordinary, Hekla."

"We just met. I'm not about to get married."

She hesitates.

"I know you think I don't lead a very exciting life but I love Lýdur. I'm no longer just me, Hekla. I'm us. I'm Lýdur and Thorgerdur."

When I say goodbye to my friend and embrace her, she says:

"If it's a girl I'll call her Katla. That'll make two volcanoes."

There's a full moon with a corona over the island of Örfirisey as I head towards Skólavördustígur.

Scrapbook two

I've finished work and am on my way home to write when I notice a girl with a beehive hairdo, standing shivering in the breeze on the other side of the street, with her eyes glued to the revolving door of Hotel Borg.

When she spots me, she walks straight over and introduces herself as a friend of Sirrí's who has asked her to put me in the picture.

"What picture?"

"Miss Iceland. She told me they've been swarming around you."

I tell her I won't be taking part in the contest.

"She didn't exactly say you would be taking part, but that your mind was elsewhere and she felt you wouldn't be a waitress for long. She said that she could sense a restless-ness in your soul and thinks you might want to go abroad."

She wants us to walk and go sit in Skálinn.

"They told me I would get to go abroad too, but it didn't happen. I wasn't sent to Long Island as they'd promised."

On the way, she glances over her shoulder several times, as if she expected someone to be following.

When we're sitting at Skálinn and I've ordered coffee with sugar cubes and my companion a twisted doughnut and a Sinalco, she tells me she works at the switchboard of the Hreyfill cab company and that the station is busiest when the boys come back onshore off the trawlers. They spend their money on taxis. One ordered a cab and had himself driven all the way north to Blönduós.

"He sat with a bottle of liquor in the back and drank. When it was finished, he dozed off and slept for most of the way. In Blönduós he wanted chops with fat, but it was Holy Thursday and everywhere was closed. The taxi driver knocked on the priest's door and was allowed to phone home to speak to his wife, who called a relative who was married to a woman who had a sister living in Blönduós. She fried some chops in breadcrumbs for the sailor, after which he was driven back to town and the boat. He slept all the way back."

She sips on the bottle of Sinalco and looks me over.

"No, you don't look like the kind of woman who stands in front of a mirror admiring her high cheekbones," she says, biting into the doughnut.

She next turns to the contest itself and says that there had been twelve girls and that there were five men on the jury.

"They had to postpone the contest three times because of rain and wind."

She sips from the bottle again.

"We were in swimsuits on a wooden platform. There were puddles of water on the stage and one girl slipped and

95

twisted her ankle. We had to hold each other up. I caught a cold and then a bladder infection."

I gaze out the window: it's getting dark and people are rushing home from work, a man clutches his hat in the wind.

"My boyfriend was proud all the same. He stood there in the grounds and clapped when I walked down the runway and did a spin. The stage was quite far away and he said it was difficult for him to make out which girl I was, but that he recognized my green swimsuit."

She chews on the doughnut and continues.

"Only problem was that I was in a yellow swimsuit."

She shuts up, brushes the crumbs off the table into the palm of her hand and places them on the plate.

"He doesn't know what I got into," she says in a low voice.

Once she has pushed the coffee cups aside and convinced herself that there are no crumbs left on the table, she reaches for her bag, pulls out a photo album and places it on the table.

"Here's the story of the contest in words and pictures," she says, moving to my side of the table and cautiously opening the album.

"This one won," she says, and reads the caption under the picture out loud, running her finger along the letters:

Glódís Zoëga's stunning beauty is a divine gift, stemming from the feminine essence of Iceland's daughters and sisters. Iceland asks no less of its female stock.

"This one won the year before," she continues, turning
the pages.

*Miss Gréta Geirsdóttir was the winner and received the honorary
title of Beauty Queen of Iceland. She is blonde and slim and graced
with great charm. Gréta is the daughter of the couple Jódís and Geir
(deceased) from the farm of Outer Lækjarkoti í Flóa. She possesses
a forthright manner.*

"This one got to meet the Russian astronaut Gagarin and to
hand him a bouquet of flowers. According to the article, he
was short and only reached the beauty queen's shoulders. He
considered her even more beautiful than Gina Lollobrigida
herself," she continues to read.

She points at other pictures.

"This one got to appear on the 'Ed Sullivan Show'
and this one had two lines in a movie about the last year
in Hitler's life. The judge in the Long Island contest said
that the name of the Icelandic beauty queen sounded like
a cascade of pebbles tumbling into an Icelandic fjord."

"What about her?" I say, pointing at a picture. If I'm not
mistaken, there's a glimpse of Tivoli towers in the background.

"Those who come in third get sent to the Miss Nordic
competition."

She continues to flick through the album.

"That's me," she says, pointing at a skinny girl. "I went
for an interview."

The caption under the photo reads: *Rannveig is unattached.*

"I was told to say that. It didn't go down well with my boyfriend."

She pulls out the interview and shows it to me.

"Is there a man in your life?"
"No."
"Are you going to get married?"
"Hopefully."

She takes a deep breath.

"They invited me to a meeting in the office before the contest and wanted me to try on the swimsuit and practise pacing the room in it. There were two of them. They said it was a good idea to have a dress rehearsal in the swimsuit before the contest to practise the walk and see if I had it in me. When I got into my swimsuit, one of them measured my breasts and hips with a tape measure and the other measured my height with a folding ruler. He placed a book on my head and drew the mark with a pencil. Then he measured the wall and said it was 173 centimetres, which was quite tall for a beauty queen, but that I could be a trade-show girl. Nonsense, said the other man, she can become a trade-show girl and products presenter once she's been to Long Island."

She pauses and looks down.

"Then the man who had measured my height left the room and I was alone with the other. He locked the door and said that I had what it takes. I would be sent to Long Island and he would be my personal tour guide. He said I would get to talk about the fire that raged under the earth and glaciers and waterfalls. To put him off, I told him I had a boyfriend even though I'd previously told him I was single, because attached girls have less of a chance of going abroad. He told me my boyfriend could wait. We were meant to have dinner together and he suggested we treat ourselves to halibut at the Naust Restaurant."

She dabs her eyes with a serviette, blows her nose and puts the album back into her bag.

I stand up and stretch out my hand to say goodbye.

She also stands and buttons up her coat. As she slips on her gloves, she wants to know if I have a boyfriend.

I tell her I don't.

"My granny made an embroidery of the picture that was published with my interview.

"It took her six weeks to draw the grid, count the squares and make the cross-stitch patterns."

beauty (in small letters)

The baby bottle stands on the kitchen table, beside half a cumin bun. As my friend pours coffee, she says she has stopped throwing up and started to put on weight.

99

"The sandwich loaf you brought lasted me three days. When you come with canapés, I eat them for dinner and give Thorgerdur rice pudding. I started with the prawn canapé and ended with the roast beef and remoulade."

The best news, though, is that she has started to write in her journal again.

"I felt too nauseous for it before."

She cuts a slice of fruitcake and places it on my plate.

"This morning I sat at the kitchen table while Thorgerdur was sleeping and the fruitcake was baking in the oven and wrote.

"Lýdur is worried about me. I can't so much as glimpse at anything beautiful, not even a glow of light in the sky at night without starting to cry. When I was hanging up nappies and sheets on the line yesterday, I noticed that Thorgerdur had gnawed a hole in her quilt and the sky could be seen through it. It was frosty, but for the first time in a month, the sky was crystal clear and, for one brief moment, eternity was in sight. I thought: *Higher, my God, nearer to Thee*, can you believe it, Hekla? I felt I could touch the sky with the tip of my pen. I felt as if I were standing a short distance away from myself and could understand what was happening, as if it were happening to someone else. Afterwards I went inside and wrote a poem. About the quilt. I felt I had created beauty. Not BEAUTY in capital letters like poets do, but in small letters: beauty. Then I shook my head at my own silliness. Eternity isn't within my reach. Compared to you, Hekla, who are the daughter of a volcano and the Arctic sea, I am the daughter of hillock and heath!"

I laugh because my friend is happy.

"When I'd written the poem, I felt that life was so wonderful that I put on a dress before Lýdur came home from the road work. He was tired but still happy that I felt so good, at least better than last weekend, as he put it. He asked me to put Thorgerdur down to sleep so we could go to bed. I'd just slipped on the dress but he wanted me out of it. That night I slid out of bed to write a few lines and Lýdur came to me at the kitchen table. He wanted to know what I was doing there in the middle of the night. 'Is Hekla influencing you?' he asked. 'Why don't you just leave that nonsense to her?'

"He was tired and apologized when we got back into bed. 'It's so easy to lose one's bearings, Ísa dear,' he said. He still finds me attractive. I told him I was writing a shopping list for tomorrow. I didn't tell him there were just two things on it: haddock fillets and a bottle of milk. Eternity is too big for me, Hekla. It's like being alone in the desert. I'd get lost. It's enough for me to camp for two nights in a birch grove in the Thrastaskógur woods where Lýdur is helping his parents build a summer house. I try to find shelter from the cold wind and inflate the blow-up mattress. I cook for the men on the primus and some thrush sings. He doesn't know that I'm listening to him. Do you know what I dream of, Hekla? Roe and liver. It won't be before January. I can't synchronize myself with time. When autumn comes with the darkness, I miss the light and meadowsweet; in the spring I long for blood pudding, in the autumn to suck the inside out of a freshly laid fulmar's egg."

She cuts two slices of fruitcake, placing one on my plate and the other on hers.

"When I fell asleep again, I dreamt I was giving birth to a child and I couldn't find a midwife. In the end I gave birth to the baby on my own. It was a big and beautiful girl, but I needed help to unwind the umbilical cord which was stuck to her nose."

I don't have a number

My trawling sailor is back on land.

I spot him when I come out of Hotel Borg, leaning against the wall of a building further down the road, opposite the post office, bareheaded in the pouring sleet. He's holding his duffel bag and is in the same woollen sweater he was wearing when he said goodbye to me. As soon as he spots me, he rushes over.

"How was the trip?"

"I thought I wouldn't survive it, Hekla. We were fishing in hellishly cold weather, the toughest men didn't even wear caps and had icicles dangling from their hair."

When we get home to Stýrimannastígur, he drops onto the sofa and buries his face in his hands in silence before looking up.

"On the way home, there was crazy weather and we sprung a leak and almost went under, the mast and the bridge were the only parts above water. We had to hammer the ice away to stop the old tub from sinking. The captain made us put on our life jackets and later we resorted to prayer. After the amen we continued to break the ice. I thought we'd sink."

He stands up.

"I was going to stay behind when we anchored at Hull, but they sensed it, the bastards, and watched me and wouldn't let me off the boat on my own."

He paces the floor.

"The only good thing about the trip is that I went to an art museum with the second mate who was keeping an eye on me. When word got out, they let him be, but not me."

He stretches out for his bag and opens it.

"Your wish was granted. I bought two books for you and a white pantsuit with wide flares and a waist belt, it's the fashion."

He brandishes one of the books in the air.

"This has just come out and is called *The Bell Jar* and it's by an American woman writer. She committed suicide this spring," he adds.

I look at the other book.

"Is this a novel?" I ask.

"No, this is a book by a French philosopher. A woman."

"What's it about?"

"The woman in the bookshop said it was about how women are the second sex. You're number two, Hekla."

He hesitates.

"I'm much further back in the line. I don't have a number."

"Do they live on their writing, these women novelists?" I ask.

"Some do. Of course they don't write in a language that's only understood by 175,000 people," he adds.

He looks serious and I sense he's anxious and elsewhere.

"We anchored in Hafnarfjördur and in the taxi on the way into town, I heard that my girlfriend had been spotted holding a boy's hand."

He looks at me.

"Who is he?"

"His name is Starkadur and he's a graduate from the Reykjavík High school. He knows Latin and he's a poet."

"Is he your boyfriend then?"

I hesitate.

"He's asked me to move in with him. He lives in a room with a shared kitchen in Skólavördustígur."

"And are you going to do that? Move in with him?"

"Yes."

He is silent for a moment and then continues.

"I envy you. I'd like to have a boyfriend like you."

In the evening I hear meowing outside and go down to let the cat in. It's sitting in front of the hall door and shoots past me as soon as I open it.

"This is Odin," I say. "He lives with us."

The sailor bends over and picks up the cat, stroking it several times.

The cat rolls its eyes and purrs.

"Odin is a female," he says.

"I know."

He looks at me.

"You have the same colour eyes."

He scratches the animal behind its ears and gives her an extra few strokes.

"Odin is expecting kittens," he adds.

Motherland

I move out of the attic room on Stýrimannastígur into the attic room on Skólavördustígur. In the basement there is an upholstery store, beside which are a dairy shop and a picture framer, diagonally across from a cobbler and barber. There is also a corner shop, a drycleaners and a toy workshop where they replace the eyes of dolls that have been damaged.

Jón John lies on the sofa with his hands cupped under his head when I come to pick up my case. The cat lies at his feet. I tell him the poet is waiting downstairs.

His eyes are swollen.

"Are you sick?"

"No."

"Are you sad?"

He turns around and looks at me.

I tell him I need to ask him for a favour. If I can keep my typewriter with him. For a while. And also whether I can come to his place after work to write.

"Doesn't the poet know that you write? Haven't you told him?"

"Not yet."

He peers at me.

"Come away with me, Hekla. Let's go abroad together."

"What would I do abroad?"

"Write books."

"No one can read my books there."

"I can read them."

"Yeah, except you."

"We're kindred spirits, Hekla."

I sit on the edge of the sofa.

"It costs money to sail. Where am I supposed to find money for the ticket? My wages are so low. And where would I get the currency?"

"There's no beauty here. It's always cold. It's always windy."

I stand up. The cat also stands and rubs itself against my legs.

My friend sits up.

"I'll come every day," I say.

"Can I mind your cat until I leave for good, Hekla? Before Christmas at the latest. Before the worst weather kicks in and the rusty tub sinks."

I hug him and tell him he can have the cat.

"Whenever I'm feeling down, I'll always imagine I'm your cat."

"I'll come back tomorrow," I repeat.

He strokes the cat.

"You'd be the woman I would want to marry, Hekla, if I were normal. But I couldn't do that to you," he adds.

The poet carries the case, but en route wants to pop into the library in Thingholtsstræti to make sure all the windows are shut. I wait for him while he walks around the building and takes two steps up the stairway in a single stride to check the door handle.

The wind whirls around the church that is being built on Skólavörduholt and rustles the rubbish. When we get up to the room, soaring engines can be heard.

"That's Gullfax on its way to Copenhagen," says the poet.

The plane waits out on the runway. The propellers rumble and then it darts down the tarmac and steel wings glide over the corrugated-iron rooftops.

I think: it only takes six hours to fly abroad on steel wings.

Only music grasps death

The poet has made room for my clothes in the wardrobe and freed some wooden hangers. Apart from what Jón John has bought me, I don't own many clothes.

"Are four hangers enough?" he asks.

There are a total of four rooms in the loft that are all let out to single men. The poet tells me that one of the neighbours is a theology student at the university, another works at the cement factory and is only home on weekends when he gets drunk on his own and falls asleep. He sometimes sobs but doesn't cause trouble. The room on the other side of the panel is rented by a boat mechanic who has started going deaf and turns his radio up loud when he's ashore. He listens to the news and all the weather forecasts of the day, to the Sailor's Station and to Sailors' Special Requests on Thursdays. Then he turns up the volume. When the batteries run out, the transistor gives off a loud hiss but sometimes he puts the batteries on the kitchen radiator to make them last longer.

Next the poet wants to show me the communal kitchen, which is shared by the four rooms as is the toilet which has a sink. In the kitchen there is a Siemens cooker and, under the sloping ceiling, a small kitchen table at which I could see myself writing.

"Here you can cook," says the poet.

The scaffolding around the church of Hallgrímskirkja

is visible through the kitchen window and beyond it, fragments of Mt Esja; a white veil of mist severs the mountain in two.

The poet has vacated part of a bookshelf and observes me as I pull books out of my case. He runs a finger over the spines, bewildered.

"Are you reading foreign authors?"

"Yes."

He picks up *Ulysses*, opens it and skims through the book.

"That's 877 pages."

"Yes."

"And did you finish it?"

"Yes. I used a dictionary."

"There aren't many national authors on your shelf," he says and smiles.

He stretches out for a book on his section of the shelf.

"It's all here. With our writers," he says, patting a cover to add emphasis to his words. "*For every thought that is conceived on earth, there is an Icelandic word.*"

He smiles at me and puts Einar Benediktsson back on the shelf.

"You don't bring owls to Athens," he concludes, and fetches another poetry book from the cabinet.

We sit side by side on the bed. He has one hand on my shoulder, while the other holds Grímur Thomsen. He only lets go of me to turn the page.

"Listen to this," he says:

"Deep inside you in the marrow
Be it joy or be it sorrow
An Icelandic song resounds"

He closes the poetry book and puts it back on the shelf.

"There's a bookbinder in a basement here over on Laugavegur, Bragi Bach, who could bind books in leather for you."

When I've finished sorting my books, I put up a photograph of Mum. She has a pensive air and peers out of the picture as if she were trying to decipher the weather or scrutinize a layer of clouds.

My wife's breast was removed yesterday, Dad wrote in his diary between two entries about the weather.

It didn't take her long to die.

One day she is baking hot cakes and the next she is gone, in the middle of the lambing season. I was alone with her in the hospital when she died. Dad and my brother were in the sheep shed. She had become unrecognizable and had difficulty breathing. Dark blotches had appeared on her skin. I lay a bouquet of dandelions on her duvet. I put my hand under hers. She was warm. Then she took her last breath and her hand went cold. The church was cold after the winter and the carcasses of flies from the previous summer lay on the windowsills. My brother sat between me and Dad on a hard wooden pew, gilded stars adorned a blue-painted celestial vault on the ceiling. The coffin sank into the grave and after the funeral reception, we went home and Dad heated some lamb soup from the previous day. My brother said he had no appetite and lay in bed with his hands under his head, staring up at the fringe chandelier. It was from a stranded ship, with painted miniature pictures depicting pastoral scenes in a blossoming countryside. One of the images was of a man with a scythe.

"Mum was forty-eight when she died," I tell the poet.

"Only music can grasp death," Dad said before closing himself off to write a description of the day's weather.

Calm. Temperature: 8°. Steinthóra Egilsdóttir, my wife of twenty years, was buried today. Thirty-three ewes have delivered. Fields under sheets of ice, horses scouring for nibbles. The Arctic skua hunts for food. Long bouts of unpredictable weather cause winterkill. Nevertheless, the flow of streamlets can now be heard resounding across the valley. There was a heavy murmur in the deep narrow channels of the river today.

"Did you know, Hekla dear," says Dad, "that it was Jónas Hallgrímsson who invented the Icelandic words for space, *himingeimur* and *heiðardalur*. It took a nineteenth-century poet to create the Great Beyond."

The poet wraps his arms around me:

"Shouldn't one get curtains now that one has a girl-friend," he says.

MORNING RADIO 8:00. LUNCHTIME NEWS 12:00.
OFF-TIME, SAILORS PROGRAMME.
AFTERNOON NEWS
15:00. ANNOUNCEMENTS
18:50. WEATHER FORECAST
19:20. NEWS 19:30.
20:00: OPUS 13: STENKA RAZIN SYMPHONIC
POEM IN B MINOR BY GLAZUNOV PERFORMED
BY THE MOSCOW PHILHARMONIC ORCHESTRA.
22:00: NEWS AND WEATHER FORECAST

The poet doesn't have to show up at the library until the afternoon so he can have a lie in. Nevertheless, he's awake and watches me getting dressed in the dark. Before I go out, he buttons up my coat as if I were a little child.

A man is taking care of me.

The morning is half gone by the time daylight finally creeps into the night like a pale pink line.

After work I walk down to Stýrimannastígur where I keep the typewriter and see Jón John and Odin, and write, while the poet meets up with his fellow poets in Café Mokka. If he's not drinking coffee in Mokka, he's at Hressingarskálinn. If he's not at Skálinn, he's at Laugavegur 11. If he's not at Laugavegur 11, he's in the upstairs bar in Naust, where the poets go when other places are closed. If he's not at Naust, he might be found at the West End Café. Occasionally, he goes to meetings at the Revolutionary Youth Movement in Tjarnargata in the evenings. When he comes home, I immediately put my book aside and we go straight to bed. Before falling asleep, I check to see the colour of the sky.

"Is my maiden from the dales checking out the weather?" the poet asks.

I ask Dad to send me my confirmation duvet. *I had an extra half kilo of eiderdown added to it,* he writes in a letter in the parcel.

"Every night with you is so immense," says the poet.

Immortality

It's Sunday and I need to get to Stýrimannastígur to write.

The poet lies in bed with a folded copy of the Thjódviljinn newspaper, *The People's Will,* on his chest.

"What's developing here is an unadulterated and unbridled form of capitalism in which racketeers steal from the people and profit becomes the only yardstick."

He stands up, zealously waving his hands about like a man on a pulpit.

"It's been nineteen years since Iceland gained its independence and wholesalers have taken over from the Danish kings and monopolistic merchants. They're building shopping malls all over Sudurlandsbraut with the profits from Danish layer cakes."

I tell the poet I'm going to visit Jón John.

"But you visited him yesterday. And the day before."

"Yes, he's sewing a curtain for the skylight."

He is bewildered.

"And does he have a sewing machine?"

"Yes."

He peruses me.

"I feel it's a bit odd that my girlfriend has a male friend whom she visits every day after work. And on weekends."

He stands by the window, hailstones pelting against the glass.

"If I didn't know he isn't into women, I'd be worried about you hanging out with him so much."

He paces the length of the floor.

"I heard about the two of you at an art exhibition in Listamannaskálinn yesterday."

"We went to a painting exhibition. Who told you about that?"

"Thórarinn Dragfjörd. He's one of us, the Mokka poets. He's read a short story he wrote on the radio."

"Yes," I say, "I said hello to him. He spoke about you."

"Oh?"

"He said you're very talented and destined to become famous."

"Did he say that?"

"Yeah."

He smiles.

"I said the same thing to him the other day. That he's very talented and destined to become famous."

He's visibly moved and has already forgotten that I have a sailor friend.

He sits at the table and lights a Chesterfield before standing up again, walking to the window and gazing out into the blizzard. From there he walks to the bed.

"Should we have a nap before you leave?" he asks. "Then there's the radio story after lunch," he adds.

"Aren't you going to go out to meet the poets?"

"Not this evening. I was thinking I'd take care of my girlfriend."

He embraces me.

"I thought we could go to a dance at the weekend. In Glaumbær. Do the twist. As couples do."

He lets go of me to go find Prokofiev in the record collection.

Curtain number one

While my sailor is sewing curtains for a skylight in Skólavördustígur, I sit on the bed with the typewriter on the bedside table and write. We're in sync; when I finish the chapter, my friend hands me the folded curtains. He had offered to buy the material for me, which is orange with violet diamonds and narrow pleats below. He puts the sewing machine back into the wardrobe and clears the desk for me.

I smile at him and feed another sheet into the typewriter.

He stands behind me and watches me write.

"Am I in the story?"

"You are and you aren't."

"I don't belong to any group, Hekla. They forgot to take me into account."

He sits on the sofa and I stand up and go sit beside him.

"Make me a chapter in a novel so that my life can have some meaning. Write about a boy who loves boys."

"I'll do that."

"And who can't stand violence."

I nod.

"They're certainly colourful," says the poet, as I'm putting up the curtains that Jón John made in Skólavördustígur. "Like a sunset and violet Mt Akrafjall all rolled into the same curtains."

He turns off the light.

"I don't mind if you hang out with the queer."

"Did you know, Hekla," my sailor had said to me as he watched me writing, "that the typewriter was invented fifty-two times?"

Curtain number two

Ísey has hung nappies outside on the line in the frost where they dangle frozen solid, I take them down and carry them inside with the pegs.

She thanks me and says she forgot the laundry.

"Remember the woman neighbour I told you about who was awake one night when I stood at the kitchen window and looked over at me?"

"Yes, I remember."

"It's been three months now and no curtains have been put up in the living-room window yet. I met her at the fish shop yesterday, she was behind me in the line and waited while the fishmonger was wrapping up my fish and joking with me. I thought to myself: there are women who are alone with children in other houses as well, and I wanted to suggest that we could take turns in boiling haddock and running over to each other with dinner before the men got home. Maybe I'll invite her over for coffee and some fruit-cake. Apart from you, she'd be the first person to come for a visit after I moved to the city. As I get bigger, the fishmonger will stop jesting with me. Then men will stop looking at me. They don't look at a woman in a maternity coat."

As we're talking, Ísey feeds her daughter milk from a bottle.

"When I came home from the fish shop, I sat down to write a few lines while Thorgerdur had her afternoon nap. Before I knew it, I'd written a story, Hekla."

"A short story or…?"

"It's about the woman in the next house. I made her walk out with a restless child at night. I made it have a tummy ache. I made it a bright summer night. I made

117

the baby fall asleep. I made the woman walk around the neighbourhood and see men coming out of an apartment carrying a rolled-up carpet with something inside it and she realizes it's a human body. The crime baffles the police, but then the woman steps in and solves the mystery. I made her find clues in the sandpit, which the men had overlooked because police officers don't search playgrounds. No one believes her. I used one line from my own life in the story, something Lýdur had said to me: *Don't let your imagination run away with you, Ísa.* I make the police officer who is taking her statement say that to her. Good job nobody knows the nonsense I get up to in broad daylight."

She shakes her head.

"I don't know what came over me. How it occurred to me to murder people. The man in the stationery shop is getting to know me. At first I used to come once a month, now it's once a week."

She is silent for a moment.

"When I get an idea, it feels like a slight electric current from the faulty cord of an iron."

Then she asks:

"Do you notice anything new?"

I look around.

No new paintings have appeared since the last time.

"The curtains?"

She smiles.

"I just got a new potted plant. A begonia."

Twenty-third night

I'm awake.

The poet is sleeping.

Apart from the vault of stars the world is black.

A sentence comes to me and then another, then an image, it's a whole page, it's a whole chapter and it struggles like a seal in a net inside my head. I try to fix my gaze on the moon through the skylight, I ask the sentences to leave, I ask them to stay, I need to get up to write, so they won't vanish. Then the world swells up and for yet one more night, I become greater than myself, I ask the good Lord to help me shrink the world again and to give me a calm, black, still sea, to give me a still-life picture with a Dutch windmill like the calendar they sell in Snæbjörn's Bookstore or an image of puppies like the one on the lid of the tin of Nóa sweets that Jón John keeps his newspaper cuttings in. I long for and I don't long, then I long to continue discovering the world every day; I don't long to boil fish on the Siemens stove and serve the men in Hotel Borg, to walk out of one cloud of cigar smoke into another with a silver tray; I long to read books all day when I'm not writing. The poet knows nothing of the seals that struggle inside me under the eiderdown duvet, but stretches out his hand to me and I allow him, as I release my grip on the words; tomorrow morning they won't be there any more, I will have lost my sentences by then because every night I lose four sentences.

It takes work to be a poet

The poet is waiting for me when I get home from work and has good news to share.

"They're going to publish one of my poems in *Thjódviljinn.*"

His poem 'The Blazing Red Flame' had been lying on the desk of the paper's editor since the spring, he explains to me.

He's delighted and distracted and pulls me into his arms. Then he immediately releases me again and paces the floor.

"I got Stefnir, the Brook Bard, to read over the poem and he liked it and mentioned in particular my twofold reference to the netherworld of Hel: hellishly cold hands, infernally deep sand... as morning dawns. He suggested I substitute one word and instead of saying 'Till death comes to fetch you', I write 'Till death comes to haunt you'. 'You only have to adjust one word,' he said."

"Yes, that has a different ring to it," I say.

The poet halts and sits on the bed. He's having second thoughts.

"Now I think I should have changed two words in the line that starts with 'assuage the wound' and ends with 'crepuscular gasping of mantled hopes'."

He reads the poem to himself.

"Then it's a question of whether it should be *mighty* or *almighty...*"

He lights his pipe and fetches a poetry book from the cabinet and skims through it in search of a particular poem. The poet has recently switched from Chesterfield cigarettes to a pipe. He reads a few lines in silence, then closes the book and puts it aside.

"I'll never grasp the winter of death," he says and stands up.

He says he's thinking of maybe popping down to the editor of *Thjódviljinn* to see if the paper has already gone to the printers.

"Isn't it all right the way it is?"

"All right isn't good enough, Hekla."

He sits on the bed again and rubs his face in his hands.

"The text is too loose. The opening is predictable, there's a lack of precision in the choice of words, it lacks depth, it lacks the pithiness of the form. It would be best to postpone publication. I'm going to ask them to delay publication."

I sit beside him, put my arm around him.

"I don't know where I stand with the other poets, Hekla. I just know I have a chair at the table in Café Mokka."

He gazes beyond me.

"I feel they look on me as one of the group and yet I'm not quite one of the group. Then I showed Stefnir the poem, he patted me on the shoulder and told me I had it in me."

I stroke his hair.

"I'll never be as good as Stefnir. I'm no match for him. I'm promising but nothing more."

He shakes his head.

"Stefnir read the first lines of a novel he's working on at Naust last night."

The poet walks the length of the floor and then walks back. He's searching for the right words. He stops in front of me and stares at me.

"It's better than anything either Laxness or Thórbergur Thordarson write. We might be talking about a new Nobel Prize winner, Hekla."

"Has he had anything published?"

"Not yet."

"Isn't that because he can't stop boozing and his output is so low?"

The poet acts as if he hasn't heard me.

He marches over to the window and is silent for a moment.

"It takes work to be a poet, Hekla. Inspiration isn't about output. Output is what you get when you work at unloading a ship or digging a ditch. Working in a cement factory or whaling centre gives one output. Constructing bridges gives one output. Being a poet isn't about output."

He picks up his pipe from the ashtray and relights it.

"A true poet sacrifices his personal life for the calling. Stefnir isn't engaged. Unlike some poets I have a girlfriend to take care of."

"Are we engaged?"

"No, but it might come to that."

He smiles.

"On the other hand, it so happens that the poets are green with envy about me. I told them you'd been invited to participate in Miss Iceland and they wanted to know what it was like living with a beauty queen."

"And how is it?"

He walks over to wrap his arms around me.

"Since a woman has moved in, I felt the need to put up a mirror."

I look around and see that a small mirror has appeared on the wall, beside the wardrobe.

"Is it too high up?" he anxiously asks, as he walks to the turntable, pulls a record out of its sleeve and slips on "Love Me Tender".

The needle rasps.

"If the poets only knew that I listen to Elvis with my girlfriend. Can I ask my darling muse for a dance?"

White

I've been waiting at the basement door for a good long while, without anyone coming to the door, and am about to turn back when Ísey comes walking between the patches of ice with the pram. She's pale and her cheeks are cold.

"I wanted to see people," she says. "So I went out to visit the painter at his studio. I wanted to tell him that

I understood him. I walked all the way because prams aren't allowed on the bus, both because they're jam-packed and because they catch on nylon stockings and make them ladder."

I help her in with the child and the pram and she pulls the girl out of her overalls and removes her hat. She sticks the bottle into a pot to warm it up and then says she's going to make coffee. Her pregnancy is beginning to show, a small bump is forming under her skirt. It occurs to me that the pinafore dress from Jón John might fit her.

"Did you meet the painter?"

"Yes, and he was very friendly. He shook my hand with his callused hand. 'From the handles of the paintbrushes,' he said.

"I told him I had three of his paintings and described them to him. He immediately knew which ones they were and said there were still jars, turpentine and rags stuck in the lava cracks of a mound where he had painted one of them.

"He also told me that there were scrape marks in the painting from the handle of the brush and that if I rub one of the paintings with paraffin oil, I'd find another painting underneath. No one knew about it but him. And me. And now you, Hekla. I held Thorgerdur in my arms and he said she was a beautiful child, even though she was grumpy. He asked about how the pictures had been framed and said that many paintings had been ruined by the frames. I described the frames to him and he was satisfied. I told him I live in a basement in 12 Kjartansgata where the sun can't be seen for five months of the year. Then the light of the paintings comes to my rescue and illuminates the living room, I said. He was pleased to hear that. I wanted to say that they illuminate my life but was afraid of bursting into tears. When he told me that the white colour was the most difficult because it was so delicate, I had to look away and dab a tear. He said such beautiful things, Hekla. He told me that unfortunately, he was all out of coffee, but that to make up for that he was going to share another secret with me, which is that there is actually green under the white colour. There are now three people who know this: him, you and me. Before I left I told him that I was afraid that my husband was going to sell the paintings to buy cement for the foundations of a house in Sogamýri. He offered to buy the paintings himself so that my husband could buy the cement."

She sits at the kitchen table with the wriggling child and is silent for a moment, occasionally casting me an inquisitive glance.

"Haven't you told the poet you're a writer yet?"

She could just as easily have asked: Does he know about the wild beast that's running loose inside you and waiting for you to release it? Does a poet understand a poet?

"He hasn't asked me," I say.

"Has he taken you to Café Mokka with him yet?"

"I mentioned it to him once."

"And what did he say?"

"He said that none of them took girlfriends with them. Besides, he'd assumed I didn't drink coffee."

"Men are born poets. By the time of their confirmation, they've taken on the inescapable role of being geniuses. It doesn't matter whether they write books or not. Women, on the other hand, grapple with puberty and have babies, which prevents them from being able to write."

She stands up, lifts the child into the cot and winds up a music box. Then she turns to tell me about a dream she had last night.

"I dreamed of a bowl full of freshly fried crullers and I don't know how to interpret the dream. Now I'm afraid that they're children. My life is over if I get pregnant again. Then I'll change into the woman who lives in the basement across the way. She's stopped going out to the shop."

Miss Northern Lights

Suddenly he's gone. My sailor.

A tremendous downpour and storm have broken out and there are few customers in the dining room. Then I spot him standing at the door with his duffel bag and I know he's saying goodbye. He says a place unexpectedly came up at the eleventh hour on one of the Fossur cargo ships that sails to Rotterdam and that it's leaving tonight. He solemnly hands me the key to the room so that I can pick up the cat and typewriter.

He says he's terminated his lease on the room.

"They were about to throw me out anyway," he says.

I don't ask him if he'll be coming back.

He tells me to take the books I want, but asks me to do him a favour and send the rest of his stuff on a coach west to Búdardalur.

He hugs me tight and says he has to hurry.

As soon as I stick the key into the lock, I hear a meow. The cat rises to its feet and stretches. I bend over to stroke it.

Odin has put on weight.

The books are in a pile on the table and, in the middle of the floor, there is an open cardboard box, on top of which I see the feathery cape Jón John has packed away.

What attracts my attention the most, though, is a full-length sleeveless dress which has been draped lengthwise on the bed. I touch the material.

On top of the dress is a letter marked *Hekla*.

I open it.

Try on the dress.

I saw a photo of Jacqueline Kennedy in this dress in a fashion mag and drew a pattern based on the same design. Her dress was white but yours is Northern Lights green. I now hear you ask: What am I supposed to do with an evening gown? You don't need a reason to wear a beautiful dress, Hekla. You are Miss Northern Lights.

I'll write to you when I've found a job in a theatre.

YOURS, D.J. JOHNSSON

P.S. *Ísey should get the sewing machine. I've included two patterns for Christmas dresses, one for a thirteen-month-old girl and the other for a four-month-pregnant woman.*

The poet has gone to Mokka when I get home with the cat, typewriter and dress. For the moment I keep the typewriter in a case under the bed. The cat surveys the room, then hops onto the bed and coils itself at its foot.

I hang the dress up in the wardrobe.

The poet comes home as I'm boiling the fish. He's convinced the cat will be able to crawl out through the skylight, down the drainpipe and onto the roof of the neighbour's garage.

He shuffles through the records I've arranged on the bed, picks one up and examines the sleeve.

"Bob Dylan," he says, turning the sleeve to read the back. "Sure doesn't look like any Rachmaninoff."

When I come back into the room after washing-up, the wardrobe is open. The poet wants to know why a long ball gown is hanging in there. He says he was about to hang up his jacket when he was confronted by this glittering Northern Lights splendour.

"And no available hanger."

Sailors' Special Requests

The poet is restless and paces the floor.

He says he was listening to the radio and by chance heard a request from me on the Sailors' Special Requests programme.

"With love to D.J. Johnsson on the Laxfoss cargo ship."

He wants to know what it means.

"I'm just giving him my support. He's so badly treated on board. And he gets seasick."

"You're my girlfriend. I'm not willing to lend you out. Not even on Sailors' Special Requests."

He turns it over in his mind.

"It wasn't even a waltz like the other sailors were getting, but a Beatles song: 'Love Me Do'. It stood out."

He turns off the radio, swiftly crosses the floor and then comes straight to the point.

"Have you slept together?"

I ponder on the words *slept together* in relation to our escapade on the geranium patch behind the sheep shed.

"Once."

"Oh, my God... I don't believe this."

He scuttles back and forth across the room, clutches his head, opens the skylight and immediately closes it again, searches through the pile of records, takes one out of its sleeve, stops himself from putting Shostakovich on the turntable and puts the record back into its sleeve, looks for a book on the shelf, hesitates and finally pulls out Bishop Vídalín's *Sermons for the Home*. Was he going to find an answer from God? He quickly fumbles through the book, then replaces it in the cabinet and struts over to the desk.

"I thought he wasn't into women."

"It happened when we were teenagers."

I think.

"We wanted to see what it was like. There was nothing else behind it." I could have added: We didn't take all our clothes off.

"How long ago was it?"

"Five years ago."

"Was he the first?"

"Yes."

"And you were probably his first love too?"

"I wouldn't say love…"

At least not *Oh, my dearest love*, I think to myself.

He interrupts me.

"Women never forget the first one."

"Like I said, we were just kids."

"And you'll always be the only woman in his life…"

I say nothing.

"Isn't that definite?"

"He also has a mother…"

I walk over to him and embrace him.

"Sorry."

I stroke his cheek.

"Let's not make a drama out of this."

The poet has calmed down and turns on the radio. They're broadcasting a violin concerto performed by the Moscow Philharmonic Orchestra.

When he has finished stuffing his pipe, he stretches out to a bookshelf and pulls out *Hunger* by Hamsun.

"Mum sometimes used to make Royal Chocolate Pudding," he says. "All you need is a whisk and a bowl."

From your consciousness to my lips

The wind is picking up, a storm is breaking out and the cat is nowhere to be seen. I call her but she doesn't answer. After I've searched the neighbourhood, it occurs to me to take a look around Stýrimannastígur, but she isn't there either. On the way home, I pass by Café Mokka to find out if the poet knows anything about the kitten-laden Odin. As far as I can make out, there is a squirming earthworm in the snow on the pavement, which is odd for this time of the year.

I make a beeline to the table where the poets are sitting. Silence strikes the group as I appear.

The poets huddle together on the bench to make room for me, but I tell them I won't be stopping. Starkadur stands up and I talk to him in hushed tones.

He knows nothing about Odin.

"I'll see you later," he says with one eye on the poets as he talks to me. They're observing us in silence.

"I found that a bit awkward," says the poet, when he comes home late that night. "When you suddenly appeared. Like you were collecting me."

He removes his sweater and combs his hand through his hair.

"We were discussing Steinn Steinarr," he says, grabbing hold of me. "*From my consciousness to your lips lies a trackless ocean*. But they thought you were cute. I was beaming with pride when you appeared in a red beret and long tossed hair. Ægir, the Glacier Poet, said you looked like a member of the French Resistance, but Dadi Dream-fjörd said you reminded him of a young untamed mare."

He smiles at me.

"I have the most beautiful girlfriend by far."

He sits on the bed and wriggles up to me. Then he assumes a stern air again.

"Stefnir's had a tough time lately."

"Oh?"

"He lost the manuscript he was working on. He managed to forget it in Naust. Apart from the opening lines he'd read to us, he didn't want anyone to see it, but said it was almost finished. It just needed proofreading.

"When he remembered it a few days later and went to pick it up, it had disappeared and no one in the place remembered seeing it. He might have left it somewhere else, he now thinks, but can't remember where. Maybe in the cloakroom of Hotel Holt. He's gone to his mother's at Hvolsvöll to drown his sorrows."

Then he turns to me.

"Has anyone ever told you you're beautiful?"

He smiles at me and pulls the *Odyssey* off the bookshelf.

"You're my Penelope."

That night I think I hear meowing outside the hall door downstairs.

I sit up.

"I'll go down and open, Hekla dear," says the poet.

Laxfoss

D.J. Johnsson doesn't return to the Laxfoss boat in Rotterdam.

The crew was too drunk to notice when he disappeared and no one on board knew what became of him. The ship sailed off without him.

"He won't get a place again," says the captain, when I ask about the fate of my sailor.

I'm allowed to phone his mother from the hotel. She remembers me well, the Dalir lass. I tell her I've put a box on the coach for her and she asks me whether I think her son will ever come back again. I say I don't know. She describes D.J. as good and kind and speaks of him in the past tense as if he were dead. He had brown eyes and dark hair, she says. He picked violets and put them in vanilla extract bottles because he wanted our home to look nice. He drew rainbows. There was nothing he couldn't do with his hands. I bought material for curtains and when I came home one day, he'd sewn them and put them up in the kitchen. He was ten years old. I hadn't even taught him how to use the sewing machine, but he'd figured it out by himself. He was a happy child, but the other kids gave him no peace. They heard gossip in their homes. He was shunned. Children are merciless, but adults are even worse.

The poetic ear

The corrugated-iron roof glistens in the silvery frost and the kitten-laden cat has difficulties walking. She no longer dares to jump down onto the neighbours' garage roof, so I escort her out in the mornings when I go to work. She follows me a long way, but then turns around. When I come home in the afternoon, she's waiting for me by the door. I boil fish and potatoes in the evening for the three of us: the cat, the poet and me. It doesn't take long. I drink a glass of milk with the fish. Occasionally I make rice pudding and we eat it with cinnamon sugar.

The poet says he's thinking of quitting at the library and getting a job as a night porter.

"I've no time to write with my library job," he says. "It's also a question of finding the right environment for inspiration," he adds.

He says they're looking for a night porter to share shifts with Áki Hvanngil at Hotel Skjaldbreidur. Áki has a poetry book in the works and says he has his best ideas at night.

"One can't create surrounded by constant distractions."

"How about in the mornings before you go to the library?"

"Mornings aren't my time, Hekla."

When the poet is asleep, I get out of bed, turn on the desk lamp and pick up the book.

Then his eyes are suddenly open. At first he lies there dead still, watching me, but then sits up. He wants to know what I'm reading. I hand him the book and he examines the cover, turns a few pages for good measure and reads the title.

He looks at me.

"Is this one of the books from the queer?"

He seems sullen.

"Some of the things you read, Hekla, are offensive to the poetic ear," he says before lying down again and turning towards the wall.

I continue reading about the second sex:

It is through gainful employment that the woman has traversed most of the distance that separated her from the male; and nothing else can guarantee her liberty in practice.

I think to myself: I have both, but I earn so little that I will never be able to save enough for a ticket abroad.

Missing you

The postman stands in the slushy snow in the skimmed-milky grey light and hands me a postcard. "Hekla Gottskálksdóttir," he reads, and I know he wants to know who is sending me a card with a photograph of red tulips and missing me. Another postcard arrives two weeks later with a picture of Frederick IX of Denmark in full attire.

Found a job and a place to live.

"I see you've received yet another card from the queer," says the poet.

Next I get a letter in a sealed envelope with a return address.

In it he writes that at first he rented a room in a B&B, but now he just rents a room.

Then he says:

I've met a man, Hekla.

Books then start arriving, one book in every parcel.

I pick them up at the post office.

In the weeks that follow, I get *Last Tales* by Karen Blixen (a postcard my friend slipped into the book tells me she also used the penname of Isak Dinesen), *Childhood Street* by Tove Ditlevsen and *Light* by Inger Christensen.

I round up words

Then one night I get up to write. I sit up, the hot body in the bed turns over and wraps the eiderdown around himself. His breathing is deep and regular. The cat sleeps in the recess under the window. The alarm clock reads five and Dad will be on his way to the shed to feed the sheep.

The skylight has misted up in the night, a white patina of snow has formed on the windowsill. I drape the poet's sweater over me, move into the kitchen to get a cloth to wipe it up. A trail of sleet streams down the glass, I trace it with my finger. Apart from the squawk of seagulls, a desolate stillness reigns over Skólavördustígur.

I fetch the typewriter from under the bed, open the door into the kitchen, place the typewriter on the table and feed a sheet into it.

I'm holding the baton.

I can light a star in the black vault.

I can also turn it off.

The world is my invention.

An hour later the poet is standing at the kitchen door in his pyjama bottoms.

The cat follows at his heels.

"What are you doing?" he asks. "Are you writing? I woke up and you'd disappeared. I searched for you, but the earth had swallowed you up," he continues as if he were way-worn after travelling down a long road and not just from the other side of the partition, as if he'd climbed a heath in search of a lost sheep who hadn't returned from the mountain and finally found her under the lee of an eroded bank where she was least expected to be found. Unless he had been searching for me in a dream?

The poet scrutinizes the pages on the table.

"Are you writing a poem?"

I look at him.

"Just a few sentences. I didn't want to wake you up."

"More than that it seems to me. That's a whole load of pages."

The cat stands by the empty saucer on the floor so I stand up, get the milk carton from the fridge and pour some into the bowl.

"Why didn't you tell me you were writing as well?"

"I was waiting for the opportunity to tell you."

"Have you been published?"

I hesitate.

"Yes, a few poems."

"A few poems?"

He seems confused and anxious.

"Four poems, to be precise, and two short stories."

He pulls out a kitchen stool and sits on it.

"A poem of mine was lying on the editor of *Thjódviljinn*'s desk for three months and you've had four poems and two short stories published. Where were they published if I may ask?"

"In magazines: *Mál og menning*, *Morgunbladid*'s literary supplement and *Birtingur*."

I hesitate.

"And two poems in the *Tíminn* newspaper," I add after some thought.

"Here I am struggling to get published and my girl-friend—Miss Northern Lights as the queer calls you—has been published in all of the country's top newspapers and magazines."

"That's a bit of an overstatement," I say. "Besides, it was under a pseudonym. I used a male name."

He looks me sternly in the eye.

"What pseudonym, may I ask?"

I hesitate.

"Sigtryggur frá Saurum."

He leaps to his feet.

"Are you Sigtryggur frá Saurum? We thought he was one of us. We knew it was a pseudonym, but didn't know which one of us it was."

"And one poem under the name of Stella Maris."

"We thought Stella Maris was Ægir, the Glacier Poet. He seemed so smug when we mentioned the short story in *Morgunbladid* and behaved as if he knew more than he was letting on, just stuffed his pipe and didn't say a word. Still, it was different from the lines he had read to us."

"The short story in *Morgunbladid* was actually a juvenile piece, I was eighteen when I wrote that. I write differently now."

The poet sits on the kitchen stool again and buries his face in his hands.

"Are you writing longer pieces?" he asks in a low voice. "I mean something longer than short stories?"

"I wanted to tell you I was writing, but wanted to finish my novel first. I knew you would have wanted to read it, but then I wouldn't have wanted to finish it."

He looks at me in disbelief.

"Are you writing a novel?"

"Yes."

"A whole book?"

"Yes."

"How long?"

I hesitate.

"Longer than two hundred pages?" he asks.

"About three hundred pages."

Our neighbour, the mechanic, has switched on his radio and turns up the volume so as not to miss the weather forecast. I have to get dressed and go to work.

"Is this your first novel?"

"I've written two other manuscripts. One of them is actually with a publisher. I'm waiting for an answer."

The poet is lost for words.

"My girlfriend is an author and I'm not."

He opens the fridge, takes out the milk and pours himself a glass.

The cat meows, the saucer is empty.

"And you've hidden this from me. I never suspected a thing. I feel like I've had to repeat an entire year at school. You've surpassed me. You're the glacier that sparkles, I'm just a molehill. You're dangerous, I'm innocuous."

My explanations are futile. The poet has been thrown off-kilter.

"Does the queer know this? That you write?"

"Yes."

He downs the glass of milk.

"And Ísey?"

"Yeah."

"Everyone but me knows my girlfriend is a novelist."

He stares at his hands.

"Did you come to Reykjavík to be an author?"

"No, to work."

He stands up.

"I didn't realize you wanted to be one of us, Hekla."

I walk over to him, put my arms around him and say:

"Let's go lie down."

And I think: let's get into bed and spread over us the quilt full of raven's feathers, full of black quills.

My manuscript

The poet stands at the desk, holding a sheet in his hand.

Mozart's Requiem is playing on the record player.

His lips are moving.

He's reading my manuscript.

I put down the shirts I picked up at the A. Smith laundry on the way home from work, walk over to the poet and take the page away from him.

"I've read your manuscript."

"It's not ready. I asked you not to read it."

The glass ashtray is crammed with butts.

I open the window.

"Didn't you go to work?" I ask.

"No, I didn't feel well. I sent them a message to say I was sick."

He sits on the bed and I sit beside him.

"If things were as they should be, I would come home for lunch, Hekla."

He looks at me.

"Would you put some potatoes on to boil like other women?"

I say nothing.

He takes the record off the turntable and turns on the radio. The ads are on.

Second-hand fridge for sale.

He turns off the radio.

"No, you don't want to be an ordinary woman, Hekla."

He stands up and props one arm up against the wall, his head drooping over his chest. After three weeks of fickle stormy weather, it has started to thaw and rain pounds the corrugated-iron.

"No one is asking you to write. Why do you have to do everything like me?"

I watch him climbing into his trousers and sweater.

"Are you going out? Aren't you sick?"

The poet doesn't answer but switches topic.

He wants to know if that vulgar guy at Hotel Borg has been pestering me lately.

"Yes, he was hitting on me today as it happens."

"What did he say?"

"He asked if I was engaged or not."

"And what did you answer?"

"I told him the truth. That I wasn't engaged. Because I'm not."

"How old is he?"

"A middle-aged man. Twice my age. Family man."

"They're the worst. I don't want to see you put on display on a stage for entertainment. It's a dreadful event: to sell women. Capitalism in its worst form. You would never see a Miss Soviet Union beauty contest? Miss Romania? Miss Cuba?"

He looks at me.

"I'm not going to participate. I've told them so many times. The man is stalking me."

He swivels on his heels and puts on his parka.

He's gone out to meet the poets.

A single sentence is more important than my body

It's 3 a.m. by the time the poet returns home, brandishing a bottle of schnapps in a paper bag.

Starkadur, the son of Hveragerdi, is drunk.

He swings an arm, falls over a chair and drags it with difficulty to the desk where he sits on it and opens a notebook. It takes him a very long time to get the cap off his fountain pen.

"I'm just a shell," I hear him say.

I get out of bed and walk over to him.

When he's finished writing *I'm just a shell* on the page, he caps his pen again with some effort and drinks from his bottle.

"Do you love him?"

"Who?"

"The queer? Does he make passes at you? Does he want to sleep with me as well?"

"Don't talk like that about him. Besides, he's gone."

He tries to clamber out of his trousers, but steps on one leg and has trouble maintaining his balance. His braces dangle.

"Don't you want to ask me what my favourite word is, Hekla? Whether it's dewy? You don't ask me about anything... One never knows what you're thinking, I can tell by the way you look that you're always writing, even when you're not writing. I know that distant look in your eyes, you're here but at the same time somewhere else..."

"That's not true, Starkadur."

"You betray nothing on the surface. When a man lives with a volcano, he knows there's glowing magma underneath... You know, Hekla, you hurl boulders in all directions... which destroy everything on their path... you're a prickly bramble... I'm no match for you..."

I take the bottle away from him.

He lies on the bed.

"Writing is more important than me, a single sentence is more important than my body," I hear him mutter unintelligibly.

I'm unable to control myself and sit at the table to write: *A single sentence is more important than my body.*

He reaches for the bottle.

"How do you do it?"

"How do I do what?"

"Get ideas."

He doesn't wait for an answer but continues:

"Has anyone ever told you you're beautiful?"

"Yes. A few people. You said it yourself a few days ago."

"Did you know that seagulls fall silent when they see you?"

"Would you like me to boil an egg for you?"

The poet had come home with three eggs in a paper bag earlier in the day.

He follows me into the kitchen and, stretching his arms out on the table, he props up his head with his hands.

"I... have been... sneaking... to look at you... while you're sleeping... to try and fathom you," I hear him mumble. "Then I feel... we're equals... When you're sleeping. Then you're... not writing... and then you're not... a better writer... than me... And..."

Listen, Hekla

When I get home, the poet is awake.

He is sitting on the bed, holding the cat, but springs to his feet to welcome me. I immediately see that he hasn't only tidied up the bedroom, emptied the ashtray and made the bed, but also washed the floor. I also notice that he's shaved and put on a tie.

There's a bouquet of yellow roses on the table, which he grabs and hands to me.

146

"Forgive me," he says. "I've neglected my girlfriend."

He embraces me.

"I was so scared you weren't coming back, Hekla. That you'd left me."

"I popped into a shop on the way home," I say, brandishing some bread and a bottle of milk.

The cat leaps onto the floor and gives itself a shake.

We don't have a vase so I hunt around for something to put the flowers in. The schnapps bottle which the poet came home with last night is empty, but there are seven roses and only three of them would squeeze through the neck of the bottle. And there's little chance of any of the hermits in the attic owning a vase, so the only option is to knock on the door of the woman who rents the rooms out on the floor below. I'm holding the bunch of roses in my arms.

She eyes me with suspicion; a woman doesn't ask another woman for the loan of a crystal vase.

"For how long?" she asks.

I could have asked in return: What's the lifespan of a rose?

"Five days," I say.

I'm expecting her to ask me about the odds of the poet breaking the vase.

When I come back up, the poet has slipped "Love Me Tender" onto the turntable. He shifts to one side on the edge of the bed, I sit beside him and he grabs my hand.

"They were asking about you."

"Who?"

"The poets. Whether you're going to pop by. I told them you were also writing. It took them by surprise. Stefnir wants to meet you."

He looks at me.

"How are you feeling?" I ask.

He says that he has a headache and that every sound is magnified in his head and turns into noise, even the cat's purrs.

A collection of Steingrímur Thorsteinsson's poems lies open on the bed.

He's already chosen the piece he's going to read to me and says: "Listen, Hekla.

> *"Of all things blue, my sweetheart dear,*
> *The best is in thy glance sincere;*
> *No sky such glorious blue has got;*
> *So blue is not forget-me-not."*

Birth of an island

> *…and sometimes islands rise out of the sea,*
> *Where chasms previously dwelt*
>
> (JÓNAS HALLGRÍMSSON, FJÖLNIR, 1835)

I'm wanted on the phone at work.

"It's your father," I'm told.

I stand with the apron around my neck and the receiver in my hand.

"An eruption has started, Hekla dear," he says. "Out in the ocean where there is no land. South-west of the Westman Islands."

He says that his sister Lolla phoned from the islands to let him know there was a lot of white vapour in the air.

"Before it was on the news. The eruption has taken everyone by surprise, she said. The day before her husband had cast his net in the same area, and now there's an eruption going on under the sea and he hadn't noticed anything abnormal, although he hadn't spotted any whales. The birds had been diving into the water as usual, hunting for food. Her friend in the east village of Vík in Mýrdal had called her the night before to say she got a whiff of sulphur when she was putting on the potatoes. They'd connected the smell with the imminent eruption under a glacier.

"Lolla says that planes carrying geologists from Reykjavík and American military aircraft from the Vellir base are flying over the area, but that sea vessels have been warned not to get too close. That means that my brother-in-law Ólafur and I can't sail up to the eruption on *Fannlaug* VE, as I'd intended."

There's a brief silence on the line and I can see that the head waiter has his eye on me. Service is required in the dining room.

As expected, my father is too restless to stay put in the west and is on his way south. He says he's already made arrangements for a taxi driver, my aunt's husband on my mother's side, to drive him to Kambabrún to see the plume of smoke with his own eyes.

"Since the eruption isn't visible from Skólavörduholt, the way it was with the 1918 Katla eruption," he adds.

"Yes, yes, Daddy dear…"

Apart from that, he tells me he needs to see an optician. His old glasses are held together with sellotape, but only just about. Now he's wondering whether he should go to the optician before or after his drive east to Kambabrún.

"Wouldn't you be more likely to see the volcanic plume if you have new glasses?" I ask.

There's another brief silence on the phone. The head waiter looms over me.

"I have to go now, Dad."

"I'll say happy birthday to you then, Hekla dear."

That comes last.

"Like I said: you were born four years too soon."

Ball of ash

It transpires that the poet has phoned his mother in the east, in Hveragerdi, to ask her if she can see the eruption through her kitchen window.

"She said she was washing-up after lunch when she heard a mighty rumble and saw the sky light up with flashes of lightning. She described a massive plume of steam to me that shot out of the ocean: a tall white pillar of smoke with a spherical crest at the top, and said that the cloud reminded her of a picture she'd seen of a nuclear explosion."

This gives the poet an opportunity to raise the subject of the Cuban crisis and world peace hanging by a thin thread.

"Mankind's lifeline is in the hands of three lunatics and total annihilation looms," he says, banging his pipe over the ashtray.

A copy of *Thjódviljinn* lies on the table with Khrushchev on the cover.

He hesitates.

"While I was at it, I told Mum I've met a girl."

He looks at me.

"Would my girlfriend like to take a coach trip east over the mountain to Hveragerdi village?"

To see an eruption and meet Mum.

End rhyme

I get off work an hour early to collect Dad at the coach terminal and he suggests seeing my workplace, saying hi to my colleagues and having a drop of coffee before the taxi driver, his brother-in-law, collects him in his Chevrolet. Sirrí serves us and he removes his cloth cap to run a comb through his hair before greeting her with a handshake. She smiles at him.

He orders cream cake with coffee for both of us and slips two sugar cubes into the coffee.

"They say the eruption is at a depth of 130 metres and that the plume of ash is 6 kilometres high," he says, stirring his coffee.

Next he wants a description of the boy I'm seeing.

"Is he a poet?"

"Yes."

"Does he write blank verse?"

I give this some thought.

"He uses alliteration, but no end rhymes," I say. "He also works at the library in Thingholtsstræti," I add. I don't mention that he's thinking of quitting his job at the library and turning into a night porter.

My father then wants to know if I'm writing.

"Is my Hekla writing?"

"I don't write as much as I would like to."

"You used strange words as a child. You read books backwards.

"You knew all those old Icelandic words for the weather.

"You said: williwaw.

"Drizzle.

"Mizzle.

"Twirlblasts.

"Thunder-head.

"Your brother wanted to wrestle and become a farmer."

He pats my cheek.

"You get that from me. The urge to scribble."

He sips his coffee.

"Weather descriptions you mean?" I ask.

"No, not exactly. What I mean, Hekla dear, is that for twenty-five years I've kept a record of people's premonitions of eruptions all over the country, including their dreams and the strange behaviour of animals."

He finishes his slice of cake and scrapes the cream off the plate.

"That's an area that geologists haven't really explored much. I'm thinking of calling it *Volcanic Memoirs* and publishing it myself."

He asks me to call over the girl for more coffee. I notice that the man from the Beauty Society is having his afternoon coffee at the window table and is keeping an eye on us.

"I don't think it's the destructive power that attracts me, Hekla dear, but the creative force."

I tell Dad I've been invited to participate in Miss Iceland but that I've turned down the offer.

"Many times," I add, "but they won't take no for an answer."

He finishes his cup of coffee and scoops the sugar out from the bottom with a spoon.

"You hold your headdress up high, Hekla dear, but don't let them ogle you and measure you like some piece of cattle. Those Laxdæla women, Gudrún Ósvífursdóttir and Auður the Deep-Minded, didn't allow themselves to be pushed around by men."

He opens the bag he has brought with him, pulls out a parcel and places it on the table.

"Your birthday present, Hekla dear. From your brother and me. Örn wrapped it."

It's *Paintings and Memories* by Ásgrímur Jónsson. I open the first page.

"It's the memoirs of that painter who painted the biggest picture of Hekla. Your grandfather was working on the roads east in Hreppur when Ásgrímur stood by the cranes and painted the mother mountain herself and most of the Árnessýsla district through the opening of a tent. He had raised a tent made of large brown sailcloth that smelt of mould—it had probably been packed wet. Your granddad greeted him in the tent and said that the patch of turf that the painter stood on had turned into a mire in the rain, a slimy pit of mud. Nevertheless, he had sensed the presence of something bigger. 'I think it was the beauty, Gottskálk,' he said to me."

He stretches out over the table for the book and wants to read the opening lines about the Krakatindur Hekla eruption in 1878:

"I'm standing out in the yard, a two-year-old toddler, all alone. But suddenly I look north-east and there, out of the blue, I see sparks of fire shooting into the air, giant red poles slashing the dark sky..."

He closes the book, looks at me, and wants to know how long I intend to hang around in the capital and if I'm considering rushing abroad after my friend.

"I think the wanderlust comes from your mother, Hekla. She had this restlessness in her soul and didn't want to be wherever she was. She used to rush out into the evening dew on her own, barefooted."

He is silent for a few moments.

"Your mother almost left me once. It was when I took you south to see the eruption of your namesake, but she thought I had taken you too close to the glowing lava."

Terms used by my father
in Hotel Borg

Pillars of fire

Ocean of fire

Beauteous fire

Sparks of fire

Bolts of fire

Eyes of fire

Cinders of fire

Shower of fire

Atrocity

A north-westerly wind sweeps down Laufásvegur and, as I walk past the American embassy, I notice that the star-spangled banner is flying at half-mast. A small cluster of people stands silently in the cold in front of the three-storey building. Unusually, the poet isn't in Mokka but at home. He is solemn, with his ears glued to the radio.

The symphony concert has been interrupted to announce an atrocity committed in the outside world.

"President Kennedy was shot dead in Dallas this morning," he says.

He stands and immediately sits again.

"Last week a new island was born. On your birthday.

"This week a world dies."

He paces the floor and says the news is still unclear, but that the Russians are believed to be behind the murder.

"People blame the Russians for everything. Not just for the launching pads in Cuba," he adds.

He puts on his jacket to go to a People's Front meeting. Odin stands and vanishes behind the door with the poet. The cat has been restless over the past few days. When I stroke her, I feel the kittens.

I need a new ribbon for the typewriter so I don't write tonight. Instead I lie in bed with *Black Feathers*.

When the poet returns, he takes off his parka, unbuttons his shirt and says:

"It's a day of national mourning in Russia. Radio Moscow is playing funeral marches."

He sits at the desk and writes some words on a sheet, which he then folds.

Is he next going to open the skylight to dispatch a paper plane with an important message about the blood-red revolution down Skólavördustígur? While the wind intensifies and pounds the window, the birds grow silent and the world comes to an end?

He takes off his trousers.

"I've got an idea for the opening couplet," he says as he lifts the duvet.

The following morning he's torn up the page.

Twelve pages

The poet has quit at the library and started working as a night porter at Hotel Skjaldbreid.

It's a slightly longer walk down to Kirkjustræti than it is to the library, as the poet points out, but on the other hand, it's a shorter distance to the Naust bar.

We meet between shift changes like colleagues; he comes home and slides under the duvet at around the same time I'm getting up. This also means that I can write into the night because I'm not disturbing the poet.

He's stopped reading for me, he's stopped saying:

"Listen to this, Hekla."

Instead he wants to know if I've written today. And for how long.

"Were you writing?"

"Yes," I reply.

"How many pages?"

I skim through the manuscript:

"Twelve."

"You've changed so much since we met. If you're not working, you're writing. If you're not writing, you're reading. You'd drain your own veins if you ran out of ink. Sometimes I feel you only moved in with me to have a roof over your head."

I slip my arms around the poet.

"Tell me, what do you see in me, Hekla?"

I give it some thought.

He presses me.

"You're a man. With a body," I answer.

And I think: He could also certainly hand me a quill like a flower

that he has plucked from a black bird

wet with blood and say:

Write.

He stares at me in astonishment.

"At least you're honest."

He lies down on the bed, fully clothed.

"A poet needs to live in the shadows and experience darkness. There's a lack of darkness with you, Hekla. You're light."

Black

The day no longer manages to pick itself up; it breaks briefly on the crystallized salty window around noon when the red sun rolls over the frozen lake, then darkens again.

"They've given her a name," says the poet.

"Who?"

"The new island. It's called Surtsey, the black island."

He cleans out his pipe in the ashtray.

"They say that so far it's still mostly a heap of black pumice, but lava has now started to flow and the island is piling up."

The poet is also looking glum because during the day the story broke that some French journalists have stepped onto the island without permission.

And planted a flag.

He's not at all happy.

"It's in the paper," he says, pointing at the article on the front page: *Unauthorized newshounds from French gossip magazine Paris Match step onto Surtsey.*

"It says they stayed on the island for twenty minutes but then had to escape from explosions and flowing lava."

He closes the newspaper and puts it down.

"It actually burned pretty fast, the tricolour. The flames from the bowels of the earth set fire to the flag of fraternity."

He stands up.

"Once an imperial power, always an imperial power, is my communist's conclusion."

He then wants to know whether I've been to Tómas Jónsson's butcher shop and bought something for dinner.

Odin's sons and daughters

I hear some rustling from the kitchen and, when I open the door, see that our neighbour, the mechanic, is crouched down on all fours in front of the kitchen table where my typewriter sits. He's in blue-striped pyjama trousers. Under the table I catch a glimpse of Odin's black pelt. When the boat mechanic stands, I count eight kittens sucking on Odin's swollen pink teats, four black like their mother, three spotted and one white. Our neighbour says that he came into the kitchen during the night to cook himself some prune porridge and saw that two kittens had already been born. He didn't want to leave the mother until she'd delivered her full litter. It had taken a good four hours and he had to poke one of the kittens on the nose because it wasn't breathing. That was the white one, he adds.

I bend over, Odin is exhausted and closes her eyes.

I gently stroke her fur.

Our neighbour said he had a tub of cream he was going to have on his prune porridge but instead had poured it into the cat's milk bowl.

"She has no appetite," he says, shaking his head.

The poet follows on my heels. He was returning from his night shift and crouches beside me to examine the furry heap under the table. He had come home with a cardboard box a few days earlier and placed it in the corner of the room. The cat had sniffed the box but shown no interest in it.

The poet straightens up.

"She didn't want my cubbyhole but instead made a lair under the table you write on," he concludes.

The undersized

On my way to Ísey's, I stop by the Liverpool household-goods shop on Laugavegur and buy a green tractor with rubber wheels for Thorgerdur.

Ísey opens the door with the child on her hip and is visibly upset. The thing she had feared the most has happened: her mother-in-law has sent her a pile of ptarmigans.

"In their skin and all. I feel like she's trying to make sure I look after Lýdur properly."

She now stands bewildered over the frozen white-feathered bundle on the drainboard.

"The problem is we never had ptarmigan at Christmas and I don't know how to cook them."

I examine the birds.

We're used to seabirds back home in Breidafjördur, so I say to my friend:

"Imagine they're puffins. Then just act as if you're cooking those."

"That's the problem, Hekla. Lýdur says I have to pluck them instead of skinning them."

She sits her daughter in a high chair and sinks onto a kitchen stool.

The child sits at the end of the table and bangs a spoon against it.

I notice there are no curtains on the window.

Ísey tells me she had taken the curtains down and soaked them in bleach, but now she doesn't feel like fishing them out again, or drying and ironing them.

"I told Lýdur I want a camera for Christmas. I'm also always thinking about the copybook hidden in the bucket," she adds in a low voice.

She ties a bib around the child's neck and, as she's stirring the skyr, tells me that Lýdur is going to quit his job with the Road Administration in the east and try to find work building blocks of flats in Álfheimar.

"He had to fill out an application form," she says and sighs. "That's new. Now the trade union wants contracts to be in writing. The funny thing was that it was so full of spelling mistakes that I had to rewrite his application from scratch for him. He says he's never been good at commas. But it wasn't just commas. He can make anything with his hands but he can't spell for peanuts. He mixes up all the letters, I don't get it. He wrote: *I the undersized.*"

She is silent for a moment.

"Will you get a man in your book to say: Being a father and husband shaped me and gave my life a purpose and meaning? Do that for me, Hekla."

I smile and stand up.

I tell her the cat is lighter and has a total of eight kittens.

"The mechanic, our neighbour, is going to take one and Sirrí, who works with me, another, but I have to find a home for the others."

I hesitate.

"There's one that's different from all the rest. White. I'm wondering if you might like to have him?"

I button up my coat and she follows me to the door.

"Starkadur is asking whether any of the poets want a cat. It could be tricky, though, because Stefnir, the Brook Bard, says Laxness doesn't have a cat."

Mother's nest

Behind the longest night lies the shortest day of the year.

On the coach, a suitcase and a tin of sweets with a picture of kittens on the lid sits above us in a net. Our neighbour, the mechanic, is going to take care of Odin and her offspring over Christmas.

"Mum wants sweets," the poet had said.

There is a snowdrift on Sandskeid, then we drive into a dim cloud of hail in the white mottled lava field of Svínahraun and the world darkens for a brief moment. On the edge of the road, up the hill by the ski lodge, it clears for an instant and when I lean over to the window and look up, I glimpse blue sky.

"There's gold in your hair," says the poet.

At the same moment, we drive into a dense mass of fog.

The poet unwraps a Prince Polo bar which he bought in the shop at the BSÍ coach terminal, snaps the chocolate wafer in two and hands me half.

"I haven't told Mum that we live together," he says. "Just that you're my girlfriend."

It's almost noon by the time the pink December sun rises above Mt Kambur. In front of us are two geologists who pull a pair of binoculars out of a holster and point them at the sea. The volcanic plume is clearly visible as it billows high into the air, like the head of a giant cauliflower, dark grey below, almost white at the top. The sight of the cloud of ash causes a stir among the passengers who huddle together at the windows on one side of the coach.

"Mum is putting us in separate rooms because we're not officially engaged," the poet continues.

After yet another bend round Kambur, the pink dawn is switched off and we drive into sleet. Here and there vapours shoot out of the earth between the mounds of snow.

The stench of skate fish hovers over the village as we step off the coach.

The poet's mother receives us at the door with a chequered Dralon apron tied around her neck.

The poet introduces us:

"Hekla, my girlfriend. Ingigerdur, my mother."

I stretch out my hand to the poet's mother.

We've arrived just in time, she's placing the skate fish and turnips on a dish.

"She wants to be called Lóló," says the poet, when his mother has vanished back into the kitchen to manage the pots.

I scan the dim living room. It's fully carpeted and I notice several homemade sheepskin rugs: one in front of a red plush sofa with fringes, another in front of an upholstered armchair, another by the sideboard and yet another in front of the closed glass cabinet that stores the precious china. On the sideboard there is a large picture in a gilded frame of a man wearing a cap. It turns out to be the poet's father, a steersman on the *Godafoss*.

She stands in her apron at the edge of the table and watches us eat.

"God, that girl doesn't..." says the poet's mother, looking at her only son.

"...eat much," the poet interjects.

"Mum, don't you want to sit down?" asks the poet.

She finally relents but barely touches her food.

"What…" she asks.

The rest of the question comes some moments later.

"…family…

"…does the girl come from?"

I tell her.

"And where…

"…does the girl come from?"

"I'm from the west, from Dalir," I say.

The poet looks at me with gratitude.

"What work does the girl…

"…do?"

Don't mention the novel writing, the poet had told me on the way.

"I work as a waitress at Hotel Borg," I say.

"Are you two…?" she asks.

"No, Mum, we're not engaged."

"Are you going to get…?"

The poet smiles at me.

"Yes, it could well happen that we'll exchange rings."

"Would you like to take…?"

She holds up a cup with a red-and-blue floral pattern and gilded brim.

"No, we won't take the cup set this time."

He smiles at me.

"Maybe next time."

All of the poet's mother's attempts at a conversation end mid-sentence.

"He didn't take…"

"I saw…"

"My Starkadur was…"

The poet completes the sentences for her.

She offers us coffee after the skate fish and brings out a can of peaches.

"Would the girl…?" she asks.

"Would you like peaches?" he asks me.

"Yes, please," I say.

After the meal we sit on the sofa, the poet lights a pipe and opens a book, as his mother brings me an album which she plants in my arms without saying a word.

I carefully turn the silk pages and glance over the deckle-edged photographs glued to the sheets.

She stands behind me and points to a boy in a woollen cap and boots, sitting on a sledge.

"Starkadur…"

"Pjetur made…"

After I've leafed through three albums, she approaches me with a shoebox.

"These are unsorted…" she says.

"Various departed ancestors from the east," says the poet who is sitting in the armchair with the *Saga of the Sworn Brothers*.

Each photo is like the next, solemn figures dressed in their Sunday best in the only photo ever taken of them.

The poet's mother stands behind the sofa and occasionally

points. "Pjetur… Kjartan Thorgrímsson… Gudrídur, Starkadur's great-aunt. Bragi…"

"Dad's brother in the east," the poet explains.

The only time the poet's mother comes close to pronouncing a complete sentence is:

"She is younger than I…"

She puts me in the guest room and her son in his old room. The ironing board stands beside my bed with the Christmas tablecloth draped over it. During the night I cautiously open the door to the poet's bedroom. He's awake and immediately lifts the corner of his quilt to make room for me. There is a sheepskin rug to the side of his single bed.

Starkadur the second

When we re-emerge in the morning, the poet's mother is boiling smoked lamb. She's got curlers in her hair and offers us home-baked rye bread with rolled meat sausage. A carton of milk stands on the table. She has also arranged home-baked cookies on a plate: butter cookies, half-moon cookies, vanilla wreaths, serina cookies and raisin biscuits. The poet's older sister is married to a sailor from Skagaströnd and lives in the north, but his younger sister and her boyfriend, a sailor from Thorlákshöfn, are expected for dinner.

"If the roads aren't blocked," says the poet who is listening to the weather forecast.

When the poet has finished setting up the Christmas lights for his mother, he wants to show me the scenes of his childhood. The path we take leads up to the churchyard and he walks straight up to the grave where Pjetur Pjetursson rests.

1905–1944, it says on the tomb.

He is silent for a brief moment. Then he says:

"Dad drank when he was on shore and was sometimes quick to lash out."

Beside the steersman is another tiny grave.

Starkadur Pjetursson, the tombstone reads. Born and died in the same year, 1939.

"My brother," says the poet.

"He was born a year before me and passed away in a cot death. I'm named after him and I owe my life to his death. Otherwise I wouldn't have been born, Mum says. He's Starkadur the first, I'm Starkadur the second."

He pulls up the collar of his jacket.

"I sometimes feel like I'm lying there and he's standing here."

Did you go…?

"Did you go…?"

"Yes, we went to the graveyard, Mum."

"Did you show…?"

"Yes, I showed Hekla both graves."

"Did you see…?"

"Yes, the volcanic plume could be seen from the graveyard."

Since more guests are expected, the dining table needs to be taken apart and extended. The poet fits the extension board, after which his mother spreads out the three-metre tablecloth she ironed while we were in the churchyard.

"Tell the girl…"

"Mum made this tablecloth," says the poet.

The electricity flickers on and off and at five o'clock, in the middle of the cooking, the power cuts off in the village from the overload. Meanwhile, the rack of lamb waits in the oven.

"It happens…" says the poet's mother.

"Yeah, it happens every year," the poet rounds off.

The radio is battery-powered so the announcements can still be heard. A communist doesn't listen to church services so the poet suggests we move into the bedroom. He wants to show me a poetry book by a poet from the village, who had published eleven books. He double-locks the door.

"Mum likes you," he says.

He's pleased.

A short while later there is a knock on the door.

"May I ask the girl to…?"

"Mum wants to know if she can ask you to fold the napkins."

She shows me where the boys should sit, her son and son-in-law—they should get the rolled-up Christmas napkins—the women's should be folded into fans. The power is back and the poet's sister and her fiancé pull up in the yard. The rack of lamb is preceded by thick, rich raisin rice pudding with cinnamon. The poet doles it out onto the plates and his mother betrays no surprise when he fishes out the almond for himself. Apart from folding the napkins, I'm not allowed to help carry anything to or from the table, or help with the dishes of roasted lamb, rhubarb jam, steaming red cabbage and caramelized potatoes, and definitely not with the washing-up.

"Because you're…"

She says this twice at the table.

"You're practically a daughter-in-law," the poet interprets.

I praise the strawberry ice cream and the poet's sister, who is eight months pregnant, passes me the bowl of wafers. The boyfriend is a man of few words, but wants to know what kind of car we came in. He says he has a Ford Taunus Station 62 model with a radio, which he bought with a mileage of 17,000 kilometres. Got it for peanuts, he says. He drops the subject and lights a cigarette when the poet tells him we came by coach. The men soon disappear into a cloud of smoke. While the mother and daughter clear the table, I look through the book cabinet until I find a small collection of poems by Karítas Thorsteinsdóttir.

The preface says she moved to the New World at a young age and settled there. I open the book:

> *I can't poeticize about Canada,*
> *I don't know Canada,*
> *Just arrived in Canada,*
> *Feel like this in Canada.*

"Happy Christmas, Hekla dear," says the poet, handing me a parcel.

I unwrap the gift: a cookery book by Helga Sigurdardóttur, the headmistress of the Housewives' Teachers College of Iceland, *Learn to Cook*. Then I pick up a Christmas parcel from Dad. It's a collection of short stories by Ásta Sigurdardóttir.

She's from Snæfellsnes, Dad writes in the card.

Sleet

By the time we fall asleep, the temperature outside is close to freezing and during the night it starts to rain over the mounds of snow, which turns into sleet before dawn. Around noon it suddenly freezes again causing perilously slippery ice and in the afternoon a blizzard breaks out. By dinner time, it subsides, leaving half a metre of snow. We had planned on returning to town the following day, but temperatures have plummeted to -10°, and the mountain road is impassable. All coach trips are cancelled until after New Year. The poet still thinks he can find us a ride and makes several calls.

"Happy Christmas, it's Starkadur," I hear him saying.

Finally he stands up and shakes his head.

"No one is driving over the mountain road until it's been cleared. It isn't such a long time to New Year," he adds unconvincingly. "A few days. Five days to be more precise."

I skim through the book cabinet in search of something I haven't read and pull out *Mother* by Maxim Gorkí. It's in two volumes, bound in grey linen and retranslated from the German translation of the Russian edition.

Cold smoked meat is served at mealtimes and at coffee there are six kinds of cookies, layer cake, both white and brown, and meringue tart. On New Year's Eve, the poet's mother serves shrimp jelly.

On New Year's night, it starts to rain and by morning the earth has cleared and it's 10°. A few rockets lay strewn in the village.

The poet has found a ride back to town. He is visibly relieved.

"We're saved," he says.

The poet's mother has referred to me as *the girl* and addressed me in the third person for seven days.

Until she says goodbye.

Then she strokes my cheek and says:

"Goodbye, Hekla dear, fairest of the mountain queens. When you come in the summer, you'll get to taste a tomato from the greenhouse."

We drive behind the snowplough in a Willys jeep that belongs to the priest, a childhood friend of the poet's who has to pop into town to bury his mother's sister. He is wearing snow boots and a woollen cap. The poet sits in the front and I in the back with a cake tin in my arms, containing the poet's favourite cookies. A patchwork quilt, a Christmas gift from the poet's mother, lies folded in the case. Two electricity pylons are down in Skólavörduholt after the wild weather, a whole chimneystack has collapsed onto Lækjartorg and windows are white from the salty wind.

At night I dream I spot Jón John from behind on the street. I run after him but it's not him. Everything is bathed in a reddish light.

Why fly,
if not to see God?

Thorgerdur is now wearing glasses.

"I noticed," Ísey tells me, "how she went up very close to things to see them. She also held on to Lýdur's ear and put her face right up to his to look at him. It seemed odd, but I thought it was because she saw him so rarely that she felt he was a stranger. But it turns out she's very short-sighted and needs glasses."

My friend stands by the cooker in a white polo-neck sweater and the brown pinafore dress from Jón John, with her back turned to me as she puts on some coffee. I sit at the kitchen table with the child in my arms.

She also wants to make me some toast with the toaster Lýdur gave her as a Christmas gift.

"We use it for guests. There aren't many of those. Just you actually. I also use it for myself and buy half a loaf of white bread and let the butter melt."

As she'd expected, she and Lýdur got a telephone side table from her parents-in-law for Christmas. She doesn't mention a camera, but says that they gave her mother-in-law a hair-salon nylon cape.

"I dreamt of Jón John," I say.

"Do you miss him?"

"He wants me to join him. He says I can live at his place and write."

"I'll never go abroad, Hekla. No more than Mum and Granny. What would I be doing there anyway? Lýdur has never been abroad either. I've already met the man of my life and know what my life will be like until I die."

"Maybe I can get a job as an air hostess," I say to my friend.

I tell her I went to the Air Iceland office on Lækjargata and that I'd been told I'm the right material.

"They said it would be preferable if I participated in a beauty contest first, but that's not a condition."

My friend peruses me.

"I know that man's oldest dream is to fly and that you want to see the clouds from above and the stars up close, but I know what you're thinking, Hekla. You can't just step off the plane and make yourself vanish like Jón John. Who's going to look after the passengers on their way home?"

She looks worried.

"And another thing, Hekla, not all the planes come back. Remember what happened to the Hrímfaxi plane last Easter. Now there's only Gullfax left."

She pours coffee into the cups.

"Besides, some of the stars are long dead, Hekla. The light takes ages to travel."

The poet says the same thing when I get home from visiting Ísey and I tell him I'm looking around for another job.

He takes a deep breath, pumping up his cheeks with air.

"Air hostesses? Is that to get abroad? Away from me?

"Are you going to visit the freak?"

Eternity is a Ferguson

"People in the capital aren't as amazing as they think they are," is the first thing my brother Örn says to me. "People in Reykjavík don't know how to work," he continues.

My brother is in town for a meeting of the Progressive Party Youth Movement and is planning on using the opportunity to go on a drinking binge and to check out the bars. We arranged to meet on Sunday morning at the Farmers' Association building in Hagatorg where he is staying at the party's expense. He's completed agricultural college and aims to drain the land and expand our father's sheep farm and turn it into the biggest in the district. He is sitting at a white tableclothed table in his suit and dress shoes, with brilliantined hair and a liquorice tie. He still has bad skin. I sit opposite him. Born on the same day as the bomb was dropped on Hiroshima, he is too young to buy alcohol or to get into bars. He therefore carries his own bottle of vodka in his jacket pocket and pours trickles into his glass of coke at regular intervals.

"The goal is to make all the ewes have three lambs each," he says, topping up his glass.

He orders a bowl of cauliflower soup and another glass of coke. With a straw.

I have coffee.

"Were you out boozing?" I ask.

He said he'd traipsed over to the Klúbbinn, Rödul and Glaumbær bars and intended to find a girlfriend but couldn't get in.

He's not impressed by what he's seen of Reykjavík, however.

"Now women are supposed to look like little girls with their body shape and clothes; flat-chested, no waist, no hips and no calves. It'll probably end with me having to advertise for a housekeeper?" he says, taking another slurp from his glass.

"No shrinking violet, mind you," he adds. "She has to be energetic and know how to drive a tractor down to the milk churn stand."

He switches the topic to wholesalers.

"They're raking in the money with foreign biscuits and bakery products, by squandering and wasting in other words, instead of boosting agriculture at home."

It occurs to me that he and the poet would have a number of things to talk about.

The next question concerns the poet as it happens because he wants to know if it's true that I live with a communist.

He doesn't wait for an answer, but instead asks me if I'm writing a novel.

I nod.

"My sister is the only writer who knows how to clear up a sheep shed."

I smile.

To my brother, eternal bliss is a solid durable tractor and time is measured by the lambs that are led to the slaughterhouse in the autumn.

He's become visibly drunk.

Finally he stands up on wobbly feet and asks me to call him a taxi because he's going out clubbing. Instead I follow my brother up to his room help him get into bed. He lets himself drop onto the mattress without protesting. The Icelandic wrestling champion won't be finding himself a woman on this city trip.

"I heard you being born," I say as I help him out of his shoes.

"I miss Mum," he mutters.

"Me too."

Then I suddenly remember how obsessed with death my brother was after Mum died. If I caught so much as a cough, he'd say there was a fair chance that I was dying.

"I went to see a medium," I hear him say under the duvet. "With Dad. Mum came through and told me not to be worried. In her voice. Everything would be fine. Most of the ewes had two lambs that year, some even three."

He drawls.

"She also mentioned you. She said that some people were born out of themselves. Like you. She sent her regards to you and said… that there needs to be… chaos in the soul to be able to give birth to a dancing star… Whatever that means…"

Winter-boots box

I immediately realize something has happened when I step out of Hotel Borg and see the poet standing by the statue of our independence hero. He rushes over to me with an urgent air.

"Hekla dear," he says and embraces me.

Then, just as swiftly he lets go of me, and doesn't look me straight in the eye when he says:

"It's Odin."

He speaks slowly, carefully choosing every word.

"What about her?"

"She got run over."

"Is she dead?"

"Yes, Hekla. The woman who lives next door said she was coming out of the milk store and walked past a cat that had been run over. She thought she saw a red van quickly drive away. Someone called the police and they came and put her down. She said she recognized Odin from the white patch around her missing eye. She came down to Mokka to tell me about it."

"So she didn't die instantly then?"

"No, not exactly."

He hugs me again.

"What did you do with her?"

"Ríkey told me I was welcome to bury her in the bed of pansies in her garden. It wasn't easy digging after the recent freeze, but we managed in the end. We put her in Ríkey's husband's winter-boots box. A normal shoebox wasn't big enough," he adds in a low voice.

That night I dream of a cat being run over and I hear the grinding of the bones and crunching of the spine, and then I see the shuddering animal crawl out from under the car with bursting entrails and bloody paws, looking for a shelter in the frozen bed of earth in which to die.

I wake up with a start and sit up. The poet gropes for me in the dark and rests an arm on me.

It has snowed during the night and the next morning a white carpet lies over the flower bed where Odin is buried.

The world is white and pure.

Like a dream.

Like a long-faded memory.

"That's spring snow," says the poet.

Some night watchers watch over nothing but the night

The poet is going to quit his job as a night porter at Hotel Skjaldbreid and try to get a job as a proofreader for a newspaper like Ægir, the Glacier Poet. He lies in bed with his head buried under a pillow. I lift the pillow and he says he has a headache.

"I'm too tired to write at night, Hekla."

He sits up and looks at me.

"The truth is I can't think of anything to write about. I have no ideas. Nothing that's close to my heart. Do you know what it means to be ordinary? No, you don't know. You've got the tumultuous river of life and death flooding through your pages, I'm just a piddling stream. I can't bear the thought of being a mediocre poet."

"Are you drunk?"

"Would you be so kind, Hekla dear, as to spare me some words from that treasure chest of yours? Those razor-sharp words that fall like an avalanche over a sleeping town."

He takes off his trousers.

"Words avoid me, they flee me as swiftly as a cluster of black clouds. It takes only fifteen words to make a poem and I can't find them. I'm sunk and above me lies the briny surf, the heavy and cold ocean, and my words can't reach the shore."

"Don't you want to go to sleep, Starkadur?"

"What can I write? The sun rises, the sun sets? I have nothing to say, Hekla."

He wipes his eyes with the pillowcase.

"I know about spring under the snow, about the green grass, about life and I know about death. But I won't be expanding the beauty of the world. I'm not destined to enhance anything."

He shakes his head.

"I'll never be bound in leather."

After a brief silence, he says:

"Now that Odin is dead, maybe we can eat something other than haddock. Do you know how to make a meat curry? Mum used to make meat curry every now and then."

When the poet is asleep, I sit at the table and write: *The words can't reach the shore.*

Thank you for submitting your novel
to us for our consideration

"You're from Dalir?"

"Yes."

"Brought up in the land of the *Laxdæla Saga*, like the poet Steinn Steinarr?"

"You could say that."

The publisher sits at a large desk under a cloud of cigar smoke and beckons me to sit opposite him. My manuscript lies on the table.

It had taken three months to get an appointment with him and I had to get permission for time off from work.

"And you sent the manuscript in a shoebox?"

"Yes…"

"That's quite a few pages."

He taps his cigar over the ashtray and presses his index finger against the manuscript.

"And you want to be a novelist?"

He doesn't wait for an answer.

"It's difficult to place you. This is neither a rural novel nor an urban novel."

He flicks through the bundle.

"There's certainly a daring and fearless element in the prose, to be honest I would have thought it had been written by a man…"

He seems to be thinking.

"The structure is also unusual; reminiscent of a spider's web… one could also talk about meshes rather than narrative threads."

"Consciousness is a web…"

The man breaks into a smirk and pulls out his cigar.

"And this young man in the story, is he a homosexual?"

"Yes."

The publisher is quiet a moment.

"It's difficult to publish this kind of stuff. Men who fondle children."

"He doesn't do that…"

He looks at me sharply, then leans back in his chair, exhaling cigar smoke.

"The fact of the matter is that this is too different from the kind of material we publish for us to be able to publish it… On top of which we're going to be publishing the memoirs of Revd Stefán Pálsson this autumn."

He smiles.

"The era of consciousness hasn't dawned yet."

He stands up and walks a few paces.

"On the other hand, you're a natural jewel in your own right; *Hekla, the crowning splendour*…"

"I've heard that quote."

"A little bird told me that they were encouraging you to compete in Miss Iceland but that you turned them down?"

"Yes, that's right."

He walks to the door and opens it.

He's expecting a young poet with his first volume of poems.

The snow crunches under my feet and a puff of white breath escapes into the cold air. Daylight is breaking. I think of Dad and what he would say. I guess he would say one of two things:

I expect you to follow in the footsteps of those steadfast Dalir women, Hekla dear.

Or: *Laxdæla Saga* wasn't a rural novel.

The hole in the ice of the lake is expanding from day to day, but I nevertheless decide to test whether the sheet of ice can carry the weight of a woman and a manuscript in a shoebox. A goose is honking.

I long to find another place,
to reach another star

Ísey finishes her coffee, turns the cup upside down, gives it three twirls and places it on the hotplate of the cooker. The child sits on the floor and plays with the kitten.

"I went to meet the publisher," I say.

"Is he going to publish the book?"

"No."

"What did he say?"

"He said he couldn't publish a book that was different from the ones his authors write."

"Didn't he find any drifting dandelion fuzz?"

"No."

"No sunrays that heal wounds?"

"No."

"No twilight haze that embraces desires?"

"No."

"No winding mossy ways?"

"No."

I say nothing and, for a while, my friend doesn't either.

"I can't let it go, Ísey. Writing. It's my lifeline. I have nothing else. Imagination is the only thing I have."

"You're not a writer of the now, Hekla, you're the writer of tomorrow. What does your father say? You were born too soon?"

She stands up and walks over to the window. Her belly has grown.

"Remember the woman I told you about in the basement across the way?"

"Yeah."

"She disappeared into the sea last weekend. The fishmonger told me about it.

"I could have figured out for myself that something wasn't right. After five months no curtains had been put up. I heard she'd been checked into the psychiatric ward in Kleppur. She'd stopped cooking and cried all day after she'd had her fourth child. She was twenty-three years old and her eldest boy was seven. Her sister is going to look after the two younger children. Her husband has a new woman and she can't take in more kids. The older boys will be sent to a community home out in the country. I really feel for them."

She turns and walks over to me.

"Do you remember, Hekla, when we went ice-skating in the valley and slid all the way back over the frozen fields? You were ahead of me and there were tufts of yellow straw that stuck through the ice and the men that eventually came west to lay the power lines hadn't arrived yet and everything was ahead of us."

She sinks onto a chair and gazes down at her hands, her open palms.

"Today the first sunray in five months broke through the basement window. I sat for a short while with the ray in my lap, with my palms full of light, before I got up."

These are the headlines:
The golden plover has arrived

The lake is filling up with birds and, before long, the length of the days and nights will even out again.

When I get home, the poet is lying on the bed with the radio to his ear, listening to the news:

These are the headlines: The golden plover has arrived...

He turns down the volume and wants to know where I've been.

I tell him.

"To Ísey's."

He sits up.

"We can't go on living like this. Boiling potatoes and fish in the same pot." He says he's heard of a room with a kitchenette in Frakkastígur that will soon be vacant. And a two-room apartment in Öldugata.

"We need to get a home that you can put your mark on. With a dining table and tablecloth. What do you say to that, Hekla dear?"

I stand by the window, a blackbird is cleaning its feathers after bathing in the drainpipe, its wings a folded umbrella.

"We could take a bus to Thingvellir and camp in a calm spot by the lake and stay there for a few days. And do things couples do," he says.

He looks at me.

"We could even take a taxi. I could borrow a tent with a rubber base and sleeping bags and we could buy supplies in Valhöll. We could get engaged."

He ponders a moment.

"I could probably borrow a summer house in Grafningur," he continues. "We could write side by side and read and inhale the scent of the flora. You could wade in the water. What do you think, Hekla dear?"

At night I go into the kitchen and roll a new sheet of paper into the typewriter:

I, the undersigned, Hekla Gottskálksdóttir, hereby resign from my job as a serving girl at Hotel Borg. The reason for my resignation is the indecent behaviour of the hotel's male customers who have been harassing me both at work and in my private life.

The light has dissolved the night

The following day I turn up at Hotel Borg in long trousers to deliver my letter of resignation.

"The world isn't the way you want it to be," says the head waiter. "You're a woman. Come to terms with that."

Then I walk into the hotel manager's office and ask for my wages for the last week.

"I expected a scandal," says Sirrí, "that you'd refuse to serve a customer or pour a pot of coffee over the men at the round table."

She stands outside on the pavement, smoking.

"I expected you to be fired for having your own opinions and not being servile enough, but not that you'd hand in your apron. Normally girls are let go if they get too big for their boots."

We are such stuff
as dreams are made on

"The poet came for dinner," says my friend.

She sits opposite me and feeds her daughter.

I sip on a cup of coffee.

"Starkadur?"

"Yes.

"I invited him in and made coffee. He was ever so sad and said we had a beautiful home. He walked up to the paintings and examined them carefully. He also looked at the photograph of us on the sideboard. He held on to the picture of you and me by the sheepfold for a long time.

"He looked at Thorgerdur and said: 'You know, Ísey, I don't know Hekla at all.' Then he asked me if you're going to leave him."

She hesitates and then looks me in the eye.

"And are you?"

"Yes."

She wipes the child's mouth, removes her bib and places her on the floor. The girl takes a few steps, towing the tractor behind her.

"Jón John sent me a ticket. I'm sailing on the *Gullfoss*."

She pours the coffee.

"By next year something will have happened in your life that changes how you view the world, whereas for me everything will be the same. Unless we grow into four. You will have stood under a shimmering leafy beech tree and breathed in its scent, you will have seen the sun shine through the foliage, there's a fair chance that you will have

190

looked an owl in the eye. You'll stand in a light cardigan and hold your coat in your arm."

She fetches the coffee pot from the stove and tops up my cup.

"You'll be out in the world and I'll be left here, hoping that the fishmonger packs the haddock in a poem or a serialized story."

She stands up and grabs her daughter who has just pushed a chair up against the sideboard and is about to climb it.

"It won't be long before the farmers back home in Dalir start to burn the withered grass, there will be a smell of smoke and singed earth in the air, black hummocks even. Flames will flicker at length beneath the moss. And when there is no longer any night between the days, a child will be born."

I have loved you
since I spied on you

Black clouds approach from the ocean and rapidly tumble overhead. A bird flies against the bank of clouds. As evening falls, the clouds begin to slow.

"Are you leaving me?"

"Yes."

"When are you leaving?"

"Tomorrow night."

"You're leaving and the migrant birds are returning," says the poet.

He looks at me.

"I knew about you before we met. I watched you. I first spotted you outside Mokka, I sat inside and you stood outside the window with your suitcase. You opened the door, scanned the place like you were looking for someone and then closed the door again. As if you'd changed your mind. I went out after you and watched you walk up Skólavördustígur. You didn't notice me. I also saw you strolling down Bankastræti once, walking tall, you were wearing chequered trousers and walked with a determined stride, like you knew what you wanted. I followed you, but you weren't aware of me. I saw you stop in three bookshops, looking at books and browsing through them without buying anything. I saw you walk into Hressingarskálinn and sit at a table with a dark-haired man. I didn't know who he was then. Everyone was staring at you, but you didn't notice. You laughed. I thought he was your boyfriend. You were different with him than you are with me. I thought to myself that I'd like to have a girlfriend that I could laugh with. I followed the two of you all the way west to Stýrimannastígur. I gathered information and found out you were working in Hotel Borg. I also asked about your friend and was told that he wasn't into women."

He's silent for a moment.

"I set myself the goal of taking you away from him, but I didn't succeed."

The time has come to embrace
necessary separations

I tell the poet I'll be staying with Ísey tonight.

"Mum airs the quilts every spring. You won't be here then."

When I say goodbye to the poet, he hands me a small oblong parcel and tells me to open it on board the *Gullfoss*.

"What I admire about you, Hekla, is that you have faith in yourself, even when nobody else does."

He offers me his hand in a handshake and then withdraws it just as fast and turns away.

In other lands no shelter find,
endless storm a-raging

"I'll never get to taste the cold buffet on the *Gullfoss* ferry," says Ísey. "They've got decorated salmon with lemons in their mouths every day for lunch, jellied halibut, green peas, white cloth napkins, hot food in the evenings, German and Danish cuisine with fizzling sparklers planted on top of the ptarmigan breasts and tornado steaks, and there are flags on the tables with the Eimskip company logo. At the captain's table there are women in long dresses and pearl necklaces, and there is a dance every evening on the deck in front of the smoking room. Everyone drinks genever and ginger ale before dinner. Then everybody gets seasick when waves strike the ship because out at sea no man is more of a man than any other. I know a woman who worked on the *Gullfoss* and she said it had been difficult to carry silver trays up and down three floors in rough seas, and she had to both help deliver babies and take care of corpses. Write to me and tell me everything, Hekla."

My friend pulls me into her arms; between us, the child she bears under her belt.

Then she pulls out a striped scarf and hands it to me. It's red and white.

"In the colours of the Danish flag," she says. "I finished it last night. It's a garter stitch," she adds and smiles. "Even though there's always good weather abroad, it will be cold on deck as you cross the sea. There will be surf, Hekla, it'll be choppy, there'll be waves."

II

AUTHOR OF THE DAY

Far on eternity's ocean
your island stands watch

(STEPHAN G. STEPHANSSON, 1904)

I no longer have
firm land under my feet

There are banks of fog along the shore and, once the hull crawls beyond the island of Engey, the mainland is no longer visible, islets and reefs come and go, floating across the surface of the water.

I share a second-class cabin with a woman and her little girl. I offer to take the top bunk and the woman is grateful. She has a Danish husband and speaks Danish to the child.

I'm travelling with a small suitcase and my typewriter, which I place on a tiny table when the woman leaves the cabin with her child. We sail south of the country and when we approach the sooty black island emerging from the ocean with its white plume of smoke, I go up on deck to find out if the rumbling of the eruption will drown out the sounds of the engine under my feet. A raft of birds bobs on the caps of the waves, and I feel the leaden weight of the steel hull beneath me. I have Ísey's lunch in my stomach, she wanted me to have boiled fish and potatoes before I left because there's no fish to be seen on plates in the Sound Strait. My stomach has started to stir and a cold seasickness sweat breaks out; everything inside me is moving, a black ocean swells in my veins.

By the time we sail past the silvery glacier, there are few passengers left up on deck. The sea churns with small whales, spouting fountain upon fountain into the sky. The surge swells, the open ocean lies ahead and the island fades in the distance; soon it will be a faint black mass under a tangle of clouds.

At night when my cabin mates are asleep, I go up on deck and lie down and look at the sky.

I'm alive.

I'm free.

I'm alone.

When I wake up, they are setting up the lunch buffet. The sea is calm with gently rippling waves, and the Faroe Islands line the horizon.

I take the parcel the poet gave me from my case, unwrap and open it. It's a fountain pen.

He's had it engraved in golden letters: *Hekla, our national poetess*.

The city of glowing copper rooftops

It's calm and raining when we pull into the port early in the morning after five days of sailing. There's no blustery surf here, no foam crashing against the rocks, just a slight nudge on the side of the ship and a glistening silvery surface.

I immediately spot D.J. Johnsson standing on the quay, waving at me in a small cluster of people. I edge my way down the gangway with my typewriter and case and he elbows his way through the crowd to welcome me. He embraces and holds me tight for a long moment and then lets go to look at me. He's wearing a brown ruffled corduroy suit and a purple shirt. His hair has grown.

"Let's go," he says, as he takes the case from me, opens an umbrella and holds it over me. "It's not far. They use umbrellas abroad," he adds with a smile.

People are on their way to work, most of them on bikes. More cyclists than I had imagined.

We wander down paved streets along the canals, passing warehouses and apartment blocks, and cross over a bridge. Although I feel like a stranger in this city, the street names are familiar: Sturlasgade, Löngubrú and H.C. Andersen Boulevard. I notice a man on a bike holding a violin case.

"You've got to watch out for the trams, they're silent. So you don't end up like the poet Jón Thoroddsen who got run over by one when he was only twenty-six years old."

On our way my friend tells me that he first got a job washing dishes and cleaning, then at a pig farm on the outskirts and had to take a train. Now he does shift work at a men's bar, not far from St Peter's church, but he is still hoping to get a job in the costume department of a theatre. He says he's got a friend who knows someone who works in theatre and thinks he might be able to get him into a tailor's firm.

"I saw Shakespeare's *Twelfth Night* this winter," he says. "I wish I had made the costumes."

I read the Danish signs and names of shops and try to memorize the landmarks: *Politiken, udsalg, lædervarer, cigaretter og tobak, gummistøvler.*

As we approach the central train station, the Tivoli towers become visible.

"We're almost there," D.J. Johnsson says, turning into Istedgade.

"This is where we live," he says, stopping in front of a red-brick building. "On the fourth floor, round the back. The entrance from the yard."

Two women stand down a cobbled alleyway, with cigarettes in the corners of their mouths.

Ivy creeps up the wall beside them.

"They're friends of mine," says D.J. Johnsson.

He follows me up the peeling lino-covered stairs, close on my heels, and says he's counted the steps: there are eighty-four. I hear a child cry and an exclamation from a neighbouring apartment, but can't make out the words being said.

"One more floor," he says.

On the penultimate landing, he stops and inserts a key into a lock. The linoleum is swollen.

The flat consists of two rooms and the front room has to be crossed to get to the inner one. The inner room contains a single bed, the other a sofa. He puts the case down on the bed and opens the window. A pigeon coos.

"You take the bed and I'll have the sofa," he says, and adds that he also works night shifts and isn't always at home.

I nod. I'm still experiencing some dock rock.

The window overlooks a back garden with a drooping broad-leafed tree.

The Danes call it a *bøgetræ*, he says, pointing at the tree.

Furniture is being dragged along the floor in the apartment above.

"This is what it's like abroad, Hekla," he says.

I'm shivery after the crossing, so D.J. Johnsson says he's going to turn on the radiator.

He has bought rye bread and salami and says he's going to put on some coffee. I follow him into the kitchen, which is shared with three other flats, as is the bathroom, and he teaches me how to use the gas stove. There's a cold water tap in the kitchen.

D.J. Johnsson briefs me while the water is boiling.

"There are a number of things you have to get used to," he says. "They eat pork and the rind as well and make meatballs out of it too. They also eat chicken. And they drink ale in the middle of a working day. Pubs are always open. And another thing, Hekla, it gets dark at night, even in the spring."

All windows open out
onto an imaginary world

In the evening D.J. Johnsson goes to work the night shift at the bar. The child on the floor below cries all evening. The moon hangs between the chimneys, and I hear footsteps on the street below, heels clicking against the pavement.

By the time I wake up, it's mid morning and a thick grey fog has descended. I open the window. In the distance a steeple hovers in mid air without its foundations.

My friend has returned from work.

He's not alone.

He introduces us.

"*Det er Hekla. Min allerbedste veninde. Hekla, det er Casper.*"*

"*Hej*," I say.

I speak Danish for the first time.

"I was on my way out," I say. "For a walk."

When I return, D.J. Johnsson is gone again. There's a note by the typewriter:

Back tomorrow morning. Write.

The sky grows heavy under a swarm of clouds and in the evening it starts to pour again, rain pelting against the cobblestones in the alley.

---

* This is Hekla. My very best friend. Hekla, this is Casper. [Translator's note]

Late in the morning my friend comes home.

Water drips from the fringe of his hair down into his collar, he has darkened eyes and a black stream trickles down his face.

"Didn't you say that the Danes use umbrellas?" I ask.

He hands me a bag of strawberries and crawls into bed.

"For you."

Dear Hekla.

The night after you left I couldn't sleep and thought of you out in the open sea. I got up and took my diary out of the bottom drawer in the kitchen (underneath the flour drawer) and wrote two sentences that popped into my head: A ship runs aground on me in the fog. While grandmothers sing lullabies over the city. When Thorgerdur woke up she said her first two-word sentence. She stroked her little finger on my cheek and said: Mammy cry. Apart from that, the main news is that the streets look like washboards after the winter. I planted some potatoes in one corner of the garden after you left. Yukon gold and red. I'm pretty big now and find it difficult to bend over. I doze off early in the evening, around the same time as the dandelions.

Napoleon's hat

D.J. Johnsson is on the landing. He leans on the banister, looks down at me and smiles. He's alone.

"I was waiting for you," he says. "The same board always creaks when you run up the stairs."

He's gone out to buy cake for me and says he's going to make coffee.

"Napoleon's hat," he says, handing me a plate with a slice of marzipan cake.

"Who is he?" I ask.

"He's a teacher."

"Is he your boyfriend?"

He hesitates.

"I have my needs. That's just how it is. One body gets drawn to another."

He looks at me and seems to be pondering something.

"It's not easy to be queer abroad either, Hekla."

He hesitates.

"Some days I feel good, some days bad. Sometimes I'm full of hope, the rest of the time not. One moment I feel everything is possible, the next moment not. I know a thousand feelings that are connected to emptiness."

He is silent for a moment.

"Here I saw men dance together for the first time in my life."

He speaks slowly.

"Some things are still banned abroad, however. Men aren't allowed to touch each other openly on the street. You won't see two men holding hands. The police also occasionally raid the bar."

I see some sheets of paper on the table.

"Were you drawing?" I ask.

"Just a few dresses," he says and stands up.

He puts on his jacket.

"I won't be home tonight. I'll be back tomorrow."

"Okay."

"Goodnight."

"Goodnight."

He looks at me.

"If I didn't have you, Hekla, I'd die."

My dearest Ísey,

I sit writing all day and soon I will have finished a new novel. Det er så dejligt.* My hosts have a horizon but lack the starkness of our landscape. As I expected everything here is flat! The light is very bright during the day, it creeps out of the straits, but there's a shortage of light in the evenings. It has rained for the past month. Understanding spoken Danish is more difficult than I imagined. "God dag" were my first words. To a friend of Jón John's. I still don't say much. I go on walks every day and have explored the length and width of the city. On the first day, I walked past many restaurants and stores and saw the king's guards and sat on a bench in a park. Yesterday I visited the grave of Jón Thoroddsen in the Vestre cemetery. He died on New Year's day in 1925. On the way home, I came across an antique bookstore with two boxes on the street, one

---

* It's so delightful. [Translator's note]

*containing books and the other 78 rpm records. I searched through
the boxes but haven't bought anything yet. The most surprising thing
abroad is the stillness of the air (not the brief showers). The rain
isn't horizontal here, instead it falls vertically like strings of pearls.
Total stillness is followed by dead calm.*

Underwood Five

Not many days pass before there is a knock on the wall and
then on the door. My neighbour is standing in her nightdress,
with her child in her arms and complains about the typewriter.

"Have you started to write by hand?" D.J. later asks,
observing as I sit at the desk brandishing a pen.

He leans over my shoulder.

"The handwriting is like a loosely knitted sweater. My old
writing teacher wouldn't give you a high grade for that scrawl."

He smiles.

"So are you left-handed too like Jimi Hendrix and Franz
Kafka?"

I tell him the neighbour complained about the noise of
the typewriter.

"You need to get an electric typewriter. They're not as
loud."

I ask him how much they cost and he tells me not to
worry about it.

"Next month we'll buy an Underwood Five.

"With the Icelandic characters ð, æ and þ, so you don't have to write the rest of your novel in Danish," he adds.

A blue DBS bike

D.J. Johnsson doesn't want me to split the rent with him or to buy food. When he comes home with a bicycle for me, I start to suspect he's taking extra shifts at the bar.

He looks up from the yard and whistles. I go to the window and he holds the bike by its handlebar and signals me to come down.

"You've got to have a bike," he says. "It's actually second-hand. But I bought a new bell for it," he adds, ringing it.

I tell him I'm going to look for a job.

"I want to work too," I say.

I tell myself I could maybe get a job at the Hotel d'Angleterre spreading rye bread with plaice and remoulade paste or peeling shrimp. Or polishing silver. In any case, somewhere behind the scenes where no one would notice me. Where I would be left in peace.

Once I've finished the book.

Hekla dear,

I have good news to share. I've had another girl. Katla. The birth went better than last time. I spent a week in the maternity ward. My sister-in-law took care of Thorgerdur while I was there.

209

It was the best time of my life. I was served meals in bed, buttermilk with brown sugar and raisins in the morning. Lýdur didn't show his disappointment even though it was another girl. He intends to have more anyway. They're just the first two, he says. I'll die if I have more children. Now I'm really worried that the dream I had—one where I was alone out on a heath and found a plover's nest with five eggs in it—means that I will have five children. Thorgerdur is really good to her sister. She's the big sister now and hands me the dummy when her little sister spits it out. The midwife came to the flat to weigh Katla yesterday. My mother-in-law says she's the spitting image of Lýdur. She said the same about Thorgerdur (I found that offensive). The sisters are nothing like each other. Lýdur has quit his road work job and started working as a welder in town. I take Katla out of the room at night, so that he can sleep because I don't want him to collapse from exhaustion into the foundations of a building. We've made a sandpit in the corner of the garden. With a lid to prevent the cats from pissing in it. Thorgerdur and I dig together and she sprinkles the sand in the air over the two of us: it rains ash and darkens. I think it's beautiful. Reminds me of you. An eruption.

D.J. Johnsson meanders up the stairs to me and the stars

D.J. Johnsson works most nights and it is often late in the morning when he staggers up the stairs to me and crawls under the covers. There is therefore no point in making the bed because as soon as I get up my friend comes home.

Sometimes D.J. doesn't work his usual night shift and is home several evenings in a row.

"The body needs some rest too," he says then.

I sit by him on the edge of the bed. He makes room for me and I lean against him.

"I thought it would be different here. I thought it was only at home that queers got married to be left in peace, but most of the guys I meet here have wives and children. It's difficult for queers to age. People ask them how come they're not married. Some give up and get married and have sex with their wives once a week with their eyes closed and listen to Brenda Lee singing 'My Baby Likes Western Guys'."

He stands up.

"Maybe I'll give up and get married some day, Hekla. But I don't want to have to lie to my wife."

My dearest Ísey,

I've started a new novel. After the manuscript that I sent to the publisher four weeks ago was lost at sea, I've followed Jón John's advice and now use carbon paper to make a copy, although it's more expensive (twice as much paper). I also have to hit the keys harder. Jón John said: Someone has stolen your story, Hekla. He's been to two painting exhibitions with me, one in Charlottenborg and another at the Kunstforeningen Art Society and also to a ballet at the Royal Danish Theatre.

Most memorable of all, though, was the concert we went to at K.B. Hallen last week with the Beatles from Liverpool. They played "I saw her standing there" and "I want to hold your hand" and other songs, but it was difficult to hear them properly because of the screams and hysteria from the Danish girls in the hall.

Job interview

I'm ushered into an office with leather upholstered furniture. The man tugs at the knees of his crisply pressed trousers as he sits opposite me. My application letter is on the table.

"It says here you want to work *behind the scenes*."

"Yes, very much so."

"It's unusual to specify the wish to remain invisible."

"You call it *en usynlige nærværelse* in Danish."

He waves the application letter and scrutinizes me.

"There are no mistakes. Flawless literary language. But you use words that are not very common in spoken Danish. Where did you learn Danish, if I may ask?"

"We still had a Danish king when I was born," I say, "and a section of our book cabinet back home was in Danish."

The man leans back in his chair and clasps his hands.

My mind travels back to the book cabinet at home. I could have told him it contained the *Gyldendals Store Danske Encyclopædi* with its 70,000 entries, weighing about four kilos, the cookery books from when Granny was at homemaking school in Jutland, also half a shelf about the history of Denmark, *The History of the Borg Family* by Gunnar Gunnarsson in Danish and *Repetition* by Søren Kierkegaard. We also had various Danish-Icelandic dictionaries, the oldest from the nineteenth century, *a dictionary that contains most of the rare, exotic and poorly understood words to be found in Danish books*, by Gunnlaugur Oddsson. I myself had an Icelandic-Danish dictionary by Sigfús Blöndal. It was rumoured that his wife Dr Björg C. Thorláksson had worked on it for twenty years without getting any credit. I read it back to back, starting on the first page and ending on the last. I actually read all the books we had at home once I'd learnt how to read, one after another, in the order in which they were arranged on the shelves, starting on the bottom shelf and working my way up. Shelf after shelf. You have to grow to read some books, Mum had said when I was annoyed at not being able to reach some of the volumes on the top shelves.

I could also have told the man we sometimes received copies of the *Familie Journal*, which were lent between farms, with pictures of King Frederick IX who had three daughters in silk dresses. *Hissing and swishing*, as a local woman put it.

"Recently, I've been reading various poetry books by female Danish writers," I say.

"Really?"

The man looks at me probingly.

"Have you any experience in *Smørrebrød*, making open sandwiches?"

"I worked in a slaughterhouse and have some experience working with cold cuts," I say.

He picks up the letter off the desk and slips on his glasses.

"Yes, it says here you worked in a slaughterhouse *forfjor*, the year before last."

He puts the letter down again.

"The reference letter attached to the application says you possess a sense of beauty and harmony?"

"Yes, that's right," I say bluntly.

When I get home, D.J. Johnsson has bought minced meat, twice-baked buns and eggs and is making meatballs.

I tell him I've got a job and that I start at six in the morning and finish at three.

"What did you write in my reference letter?" I ask my friend.

My dear Hekla,

Thank you for the coat for Thorgerdur. No other child in the neighbourhood owns such a fine garment. We bought a lawnmower and I went out to cut the grass at four o'clock in the morning. I kept the door half open but the girls were fast asleep. And their father too. I hadn't written in the diary over the past weeks, but when I came in I wrote three sentences: "The grass is so tall that it reaches my nipples. It's on the limit of being able to continue growing vertically. Then it will lie down like a woman giving birth." It wasn't really like that, though, because the grass barely reached my ankles. But I longed to mention my nipples. Probably because my breasts are so

214

full of milk. If I had described the lawn after I had mowed it, I could have used a male simile and spoken about stubble. After writing those three sentences, I decided to stop writing in the diary. I've packed away my wings. They were a small bird's wings that could carry me no further than east to the birch grove of Thrastaskógur, oh, Hekla. The other main news is that one of the twins in the fish shop died (unexpectedly) and I don't know which one it was. The one who survived doesn't tease me, but I don't know whether that's because he's mourning his brother or because it was the one who called me his darling who died. I'm a 22-year-old mother of two and there's a streak of melancholic nostalgia inside me. Sorry for sharing these thoughts with you. Throw away these squiggles.

Have I travelled far away enough
from home to cry?

D.J. Johnsson hasn't come home for two days.

"He's off this weekend," says his colleague when I enquire about him at the bar. He looks me over as he dries the glasses.

"Are you his sister? You resemble each other like two drops of water. Except he's dark and you're blonde."

When D.J. Johnsson finally returns, he's wobbling on his feet, clutching a bottle of beer. He looks like he hasn't slept.

I stare at him.

"I'm not selling myself," he says. "I don't do drugs. I'm celebrating being alive."

I sit beside him on the bed.

"You know, Hekla, some men want me to dress up and play a woman. I don't want to be treated like a woman, Hekla. I'm a man."

"I know."

He droops his head.

"I'm just a guy who likes guys."

He lies on the bed and presses the pillow against his head. I sit with him and stroke him. He's shaking.

"I'm a foreigner in this flat country. D.J. Johnsson. I'm a guest on this earth. I was born by accident. I wasn't planned for. Sometimes I'm so tired, Hekla. Of existing and sometimes

"I just want to

"Sleep

"nod off

"conk out

"for a whole month."

I try to remember if we have any leftover herring and beetroot.

"Shall I make you some *smørrebrød*?" I ask.

"I want to sew, Hekla. The sewing machine is my typewriter."

Hekla dear,

The day has turned into night. Temperature: 9°. It looks as if the hay harvest will be reasonable, despite the wet, windy spring. It would have made a difference to have you with us in the haymaking, unlike some poets who are too feeble for outdoor work. It's actually quite amazing how so many poets lack physical stamina. If they're not blind like Homer, Milton and Borges, they're lame and can't do any sort of labour. Once a poet from Reykjavík joined us for six days, a distant cousin of your mother's, whom she pampered, of course. At the peak of the haymaking season. His mission was to listen to the vernacular of country folk while we were working.

Apart from that, the main news is that the eruption in Surtsey continues. It has been going on for nine months now and the island has grown to a height of 174 metres. In the spring, two new craters opened beside the mother island and two extra islands were formed. They were named Surtur the first and Surtur the second in the royalist tradition. And it's not all over because yet another island is expected to be born from a small black crater that has been named Syrtling.

Then the July nights arrived, warm and silent. All days pass, all moments vanish.

YOUR FATHER

So far from the battlefield of the world

"I could," says D.J. Johnsson, seemingly giving it some thought, "ask a friend of mine to read it over if you want to try to write in Danish."

"Like Gunnar Gunnarsson?"

"I was thinking more of a short story maybe."

That night he climbs into the bed.

"It was cold out there.

"And I was lonely," he adds.

I make room for him.

"I dreamt," he says, "that I was on a merry-go-round in a deserted Tivoli Gardens, in a bleak barren landscape. I was alone and I thought: the world spins with everything but me."

He hesitates.

"I think, Hekla, that I want to be buried beside Mum, in the west in Búdardalur."

My dearest Hekla,

We've got a patch of land in Sogamýri. Lýdur goes there every evening to work on the foundations. Then I'm alone with the girls. He's going to join the Lions or Kiwanis club. It's the only way, he says. A family man with a wife and two children has to have connections. Otherwise you won't get any builders. Lýdur is really happy with his girls and I've got to give it to him, he's good at sleeping through the children crying at night. He's also understanding about the mess the apartment is in. I'm making Lýdur a pair of trousers with the sewing machine Jón John gave me, but it's more difficult than it seems.

Burn this letter in a fire. No, tear it to shreds, scatter it in the air and let it snow on you, dearest friend, and fall on your shoulders. You don't have to be naked.

YOUR BEST FRIEND (FOR LIFE)

South

"We're losing the flat in the autumn," says D.J. Johnsson. "What should we do then?"

I finish the sentence I'm writing and turn.

"We'll find another flat."

He looks at me.

"Let's go away, Hekla."

I stand up.

"Where to?"

"South. By train."

He's standing in the middle of the floor.

"We're two of a kind, Hekla. Neither of us is at home anywhere."

"We don't have the money for a train ticket. We don't own anything."

I think: my only possessions are two typewriters, one of which is electric.

"We'll find a way. I'll take on more shifts."

He muses.

"It'll take us a week to travel and you can write."

"All the way?"

"Yes, all the way. We'll travel as far as the train can take us, until we reach the sea. On the journey we'll buy bread and cheeses named after the villages they're made in."

Dear Hekla,

I have news to share. We just bought a car, to be more precise: an orange Saab that Lýdur got as a bargain through his brother-in-law. And not only that, but I now have a driver's licence. Lýdur encouraged me to and took me on several drives to save on the driving lessons. The driving instructor was really surprised I knew how to reverse. In the test I had to park the car. Neither Mum nor my mother-in-law has a driving licence. I wanted to drive to Sogamýri on my first drive to see Lýdur working on the foundations, but I got no further than Snorrabraut where I almost backed into a tourist. He wasn't hurt but we were both equally startled. Who expects to find a tourist in the country in the second half of August? He turned out to be a French geologist, who'd come here because of the Surtsey eruption. He had a map and pointed out where he was going. I felt the least I could do was drive him to Thorlákshöfn even though I had the two girls in the back. Fortunately, Katla slept in the carrycot for most of the way. Otherwise I would have had to stop at the ski shelter to breastfeed her. It took a while to explain to him that my friend was called Hekla and my daughter Katla, but he got it in the end.

They're two volcanoes, I said.

P.S. *I saw Starkadur on Barónsstígur yesterday with a girl. I think I spotted engagement rings. He asked whether I'd received any mail from you and I said that I got a letter every week. He peeped into the pram. His girlfriend was all wide-eyed during the conversation.*

There are two people inside me
and they are at war with each other

D.J. Johnsson is waiting for me after work and accompanies me home. He rides his bike and I mine, and I immediately sense he is on edge.

"Is something up?"

He gets straight to the point.

"I was wondering, Hekla, whether it wouldn't be better to get married before the trip."

I look at him, he seems worried.

I smile at him.

He strokes the fringe over his eyes.

"I'm serious, Hekla."

This is the third time he mentions marriage in a short period, either because some friend of his is about to get married or he believes he'll eventually end up getting married.

"Does that mean you're going to give up?"

He doesn't answer the question but looks straight into the distance.

"I've been thinking about it for some time. It could be useful for both of us."

He hesitates.

"It's also cheaper. We only need one hotel room if we have wedding rings."

"It would never work," I say.

"There are many different types of marriages," he continues. "You're my best friend. We're both misfits."

He stops and looks at me.

"It wouldn't change anything. I'd get to be myself and you'd get to write. We'd take care of each other."

We approach the hall door. He helps me lock my bike.

"It's not as if I haven't been propositioned by women," he says.

Two dogs start fighting in the alleyway.

"We'd make a pretty couple. We'd make the most beautiful couple, Hekla."

My dearest Hekla,

My father-in-law died two weeks ago after a difficult illness. I wrote an obituary about him in Morgunbladid. It was the only eulogy. Even though he hadn't been close to Lýdur, I felt he deserved the article for the Kjarval paintings. Lýdur embraced me that evening and said that he never knew that his father had been a fan of Hannes Hafsteinn's poetry. (He had asked me to read the article to him because for some reason the letters became all jumbled when he tried to read it himself. I don't understand why.) I based it on the lines: "I love you, storm, I love you, love you, eternal battle." What was heartbreaking for Lýdur, however, was that there was a woman with a black veil sitting in the church that no one seemed to recognize. She seemed so devastated. Lýdur says he can't figure it out. I pulled myself together and made some curtains with the sewing machine. They're orange like the Saab. Lýdur didn't notice any change in the bedroom.

*P.S. I read the Sylvia Plath poem you sent me and it changed every-
thing, I'm not the same person as I was before because it was about
me. It was so strange and beautiful, thank you for translating it for
me; I haven't been able to think of anything else.*

Nebula

I've written to the editors of three newspapers in Iceland to
ask them if I can send them travel pieces. I would preferably
need to be paid in advance. When we're on the point of
giving up on the idea of the trip, three things happen: I get
an answer from the editor of *Alþýdublað* who is willing to pay
for my articles and give me a small advance. Then I also
get a letter from a Danish editor who wants to publish a
short story I had sent him and which Jón John's colleague
at the bar had read over for me. The letter said the structure was unusual and *reminiscent of nebula. But there is a system
"i galskabet", method in your madness*, he writes. The letter is
accompanied by a cheque. I fetch the bike and cycle straight
to the station to buy two train tickets. One way.

But the greatest difference to the travel fund came from
the contents of Dad's letter.

Hekla dear,
    *The summer has been its usual self. Neither dry nor raining at
the right time. You write to say you're thinking of taking a journey*

down south. Won't you be needing some pocket money then? Enclosed is a stamped letter that your mother had in her belongings and which is from a pile of letters handed down by her great-grandfather. It's a reply from a royal official to a letter of complaint her great-grandfather had written about a magistrate's unauthorized expropriation of eggs from his land. It occurred to me, Hekla dear, that you might be able to make some money out of it. Stamps are considered more valuable if they are still on the envelope. That's all I have to say but hope that your trip down south will be educational and satisfactory.

Hotel Beach

We step off the train late at night. It's still dark so we sit on a bench in the waiting room of the station, waiting for the fireball to rise above the curved horizon and the world to assume a form. Then we take our cases and walk down to the beach and lie in the sand. And fall asleep.

I awake with sand in my hair, shell fragments in the hollows of my knees and heat on my eyelids; a white light fills every corner of the world. I taste salt on my lips. A man comes running over with two parasols and plants them in the sand beside us.

I fall asleep again.

When I open my eyes, I see D.J. Johnsson standing dead still on the edge of the shore, staring straight out at the sea. He still has on the same white suit he was wearing when we started our journey five days ago; his trousers rolled up. I see him wading out into the water and walk over to him, bend and plant my hands in the water, which gushes between my fingers, leaving them salted. Then I turn again. The beach gradually fills with people; children dig holes in the sand and women massage their men with oil. They have baskets from which they pull out towels and sun hats.

The heat hits me.

I've no experience of such high temperatures, apart from one day seven years ago at the peak of the harvest when there was a heat wave in Dalir and temperatures hit 26°. My father undid one button of his flannel shirt: a line at the bottom of his neck marked the beginning of his snow-white torso.

I lose sight of D.J. Johnsson, but suddenly he's standing beside me holding two ice pops.

"Let's go," he says.

I notice that men aren't just looking at me, but also at my friend. And he at them.

"Don't say anything and don't look back," he says as he stretches out his hand and hoists me to my feet.

My dear Ísey,

I have some news to give you. Jón John and I are going on a trip. After the rainiest summer in the city in human memory, we decided to move south. We gave up our jobs and flat, I sold my electric typewriter for a pittance to an Icelandic Nordic Studies student and we packed two small suitcases. I'd never stepped onto a train before and experienced the world in movement while I sat still. Don't be shocked, Ísey dear, but Jón John and I got married in the city hall before we set off. So I am now a married woman. It was a beautiful but short ceremony. We bought two golden rings. Jón John was wearing a white suit and I the Northern Lights dress which he'd sewn for me last year, but which I hadn't had a chance to wear. The best men were Jón John's friend who is a teacher and Mette who worked with me at the Smørrebrød department. We bought a marzipan tart and Mette brought some sweet white wine and we sat down on a park bench and drank it. Don't worry, Jón John understands me and my need to write, and we take care of each other. I'm strong and he is vulnerable, but he protects me in his own way.

    Your friend,

    HEKLA

This is where we'll stop

The train is still on the track in the middle of a valley and then slowly crawls into the station. My husband tells me that the train station is named after a freedom fighter who was executed.

This is the first destination.

We scan the menu prices of a restaurant and in the end buy some bread and slices of sausage. We hesitate in front of the cheese, it's too expensive.

The woman who runs the Saint Lucy guest house with her husband takes her time registering the information from our passports. She's also slow to browse through the blank pages, as if she were trying to decide whether to rent us the room or not. It's half board. Occasionally, she looks up to inspect us. On the table beside her stands the statue of a haloed woman who in her outstretched hand holds out her eyes on a plate. I glance at D.J. Johnsson and wonder if he's trying to imagine what the woman is thinking; is she maybe wondering whether he will be lying on top of his wife tonight?

While the woman busies herself with the paperwork, we scan our surroundings.

In the dining room a television blares at full volume: four stations, explains the woman who is keeping one eye on us and holds up four fingers. The set radiates a blue glow onto the street. On the tables are chequered tablecloths and plastic flowers in vases, and the chairs have been arranged so that everyone can see the television screen while they're eating. I flaunt the wedding ring and in the end the woman hands my husband a key to a room with light green walls. The cold bedclothes are damp and the wardrobe is full of hangers. My husband hangs his jacket on one of them, unbuttons his shirt and lies on the bed. The sound carries well in the heat: a conversation from two floors below us can be heard as if it were being whispered into our ears, somewhere down on the street a man is singing. I open the shutters in front of the window, the street is so narrow that one can barely catch a glimpse of the sky, the guest house's bedsheets are hanging out to dry on a line that stretches across the street.

"You can marry another man later," I hear from the bed.

I turn around.

"I don't want another man," I say.

I lie on the bed beside him.

"You're the only man who places no demands on me."

He lies with his arms stretched down by his sides. With upturned palms. I stroke the lifeline with my finger. It's powerful but ends abruptly.

"Do you think we'll survive this?" he asks.

"Yes, we will.

"If not the two of us, then another two."

He stands up.

"I've written to Mum and told her I'm a married man."

My dear Hekla,

I hope you won't resent me writing to you because you still have and will always have a place in my heart. I hope this is the right address—I got it from Ísey.

The last time I wrote to you, the letter was returned to me with "not at this address" written on the envelope. Now I'm relieved you didn't get that letter because it was too mawkish. It had been written soon after you'd sailed away and there was too much moaning in it. My thoughts were all about you. My circumstances have changed since then and I've met a girl from Mýrdalir and have started driving a taxi. I've stopped writing poetry because I have nothing to say. Now I drive poets home from bars. More often than not I work twelve-hour shifts and sometimes weekends too. I heard about your manuscript in Mokka. Áki Hvanngil had read it as well as some others. Áki got the manuscript from one of his sister's neighbours who knows the publisher's reader. There's one thing I want to say to you, Hekla: you have a gift. You have courage. Even though I'm no longer a poet, I can recognize writing talent when I see it.

I'll never forget you.

Your eternal friend,

STARKADUR PJETURSSON

A hole has appeared in the night

My husband has one pillow and I the other, but we share the same sheet. Sometimes we both lie on our backs or he lies on his back and I lie on my stomach, other times we turn our backs on each other. Occasionally I hold him like a sister holds a brother or he holds me like a friend holds a friend. He doesn't leave a hand clutching the woman's breast on the other side of the bed. Nevertheless, when I wake up, it takes a moment to remember that the male body lying beside me is one that only men are allowed to touch.

I wake up once during the night and my husband isn't there. I fall asleep again and when I awaken he's standing in the middle of the room and looking at me and smiling. He hands me a cup of coffee and a slice of cake. We help each other spread the clammy, crumpled sheet, stretch it over the mattress and then tuck in the corners.

The sky is as blue as yesterday and D.J. Johnsson suggests we go and take a look at an old church. There's a damp smell inside like in an old potato larder. D.J. walks ahead of me and halts in front of a painting of a young man with golden locks spilling over his shoulders, with his hands tied behind his back and his eyes gazing up at the heavens. A multitude of arrows pierce his stunning body.

I rest my head on D.J. Johnsson's shoulder.

"You can't get close to a saint without burning your fingertips," I say.

He contemplates the work.

"I wish I were normal, Hekla. I wish I weren't me."

When we get back, the woman tells us a room has been freed on the other side of the guest house with a view of the hills. She says she's willing to give it to us because we're on our honeymoon. She was sitting at the television with her husband, both when we left and when we return, and I notice that she asks him if he wants some peach as she holds out a slice to him on the tip of her knife.

Do not awaken love
until it so desires

There is a small back garden by the guest house with some plastic chairs and a table. That is where I go with my old typewriter to avoid waking up my friend who came back late last night. There is a pink streak of light in the sky which has vanished by the time I pull the first sheet out of the typewriter.

The manager's husband walks by in a white T-shirt and nods at me.

"Lady novelist," he says.

It's an affirmation. A deduction. He's been pondering on this for several days.

"You're getting a tan," I hear from the bed when I get back.

"You're breaking out in freckles. You're turning golden."

I'm getting a slight tan from sitting and digging in the sandpit, Ísey wrote this summer. *Even though it's always windy and the sun is cold. Thorgerdur has had a cold all summer.*

Dearest Ísey,

The heat seeps in everywhere. The nights are hot as well (even though the floor tiles are ice cold). I've tasted various fruits that can't be found at home, such as grapes and peaches. Maybe I'll become a wholesaler and import fruit for Thorgerdur and Katla. (But it would probably be a hopeless enterprise while all the foreign currency goes into buying fuel for the fishing ships.) Yesterday we ate octopus. They're as chewy as rubber. I write eight hours a day. The senses are sharpest in the moment just before the sudden fall of darkness. Like carved marble. Jón John has been better than I have at getting to know the locals. Last night I dreamt that there were too many words in the world, but that there was a shortage of bodies. We'll stay here for as long as the money lasts.

P.S. I got a letter from Starkadur who tells me my manuscript has been circulating (the one that was lost at sea) and that several people have read it. I'm far into a new novel that is different from anything else I've written. I don't expect anyone will want to publish it any more than the other ones.

Peace

When my husband gets home, he's holding a bottle of wine in his hands.

He places it on the table, then pulls a pair of sunglasses out of his pocket and hands them to me.

"For you."

I close the book. He borrows wine glasses from the manager.

He has news.

"Martin Luther King won the Nobel Peace prize yesterday."

He had sat with the couple who run the guest house and watched television and the woman had helped him to understand the news. *Black*, she repeated several times, pointing at the colour of the skirt she was wearing. *Peace*.

"Did you know, Hekla, that several queers have been awarded the Nobel Prize for literature?

"Selma Lagerlöf, Thomas Mann, André Gide…" He trails off.

He does not kiss me with the kisses of his mouth

"Are you reading the Bible?"

He is bewildered.

"Yes, it was in the bedside table."

"Do you understand the language?"

"No, but I know the Song of Songs off by heart."

I put the book back in its place.

"I got a letter from Dad," I say, indicating an envelope that is lying on the table.

He stands up and walks over to me.

"Does he want to know if I'm capable of performing my male function?"

I take the letter out of the thin envelope and unfold it.

"He says he's heard about my changed circumstances and asks whether there might not be some obstacles to the match."

I hesitate.

"He says we're not a likely couple."

My husband sits on the bed and buries his face in his hands.

"Forgive me," I hear him say between his fingers.

"Forgive you for what?"

"Forgive me for not being the man that you need. For not being able to love a woman."

He stands up, opens the wardrobe, pulls out a yellow shirt and puts it on. He looks at me as he buttons it up.

"It sometimes happens that I think of women and their bodies. About you. For a brief moment. Then I go back to thinking about men and their bodies."

In my bed at night I sought him
but did not find him

I wake up in the middle of the night and reach for my husband in the bed. I'm alone. I fall back asleep. When I wake in the morning, he's lying beside me. Fully dressed. In the same clothes as yesterday. Daylight filters through the shutter. He sits up and looks straight ahead. Into the darkness.

I get up and open the shutters.

He looks battered and says he got into a scuffle. He'd been down at the train station, the police had come and arrested some men in the toilets.

"Are you putting yourself in danger?" I ask.

He seems to be mulling this over.

"I can't behave sensibly, Hekla," he finally says.

I ask him how it works when he goes out to meet other men.

"You let them know you're interested. That's all there is to it. It's not complicated."

I sit beside him.

"Most of the men I meet are married."

"Like you?"

He looks at me.

"Yeah, like me."

"So you understand each other?" I say.

"I give them what they don't get from their wives."

"Except you don't have to sleep with your wife."

He clasps his head with both hands.

"I know I have nothing to offer you, Hekla."

He stands up and takes off his crumpled trousers and shirt.

Then he rinses his face in cold water at the basin in the corner of the room. I notice he's looking at me in the mirror.

"What are you thinking about?" I ask.

"About you and your book and whether I'm a minor character or a main character in it, and about a man I met yesterday, and about Mum and what she might be doing, and about a dream I dreamt last night."

He turns to me.

"The dream was like a memory of a winter's day in Dalir. Everything was so pure. It was all so white. Snow white. It was still, Hekla. And the weird thing was that it was warm. It was silent. Totally silent. As if I were dead."

What never happened

I sit at the table and I think he is still lying in bed, but suddenly he's standing at my shoulder and watching me write. I turn around.

"What do you look forward to?" he asks.

"I look forward to finishing the book I'm writing."

"And then?"

"To starting a new book."

"And then?"

"To writing another book."

"And when you finish that?"

I hesitate.

"I don't know.

"And you?"

He walks to the window and turns his back to me.

"Make us lovers in the story, Hekla. Make what isn't going to happen happen. Let the words become flesh. Make me a father. So that I leave something behind."

"The world won't always be like this," I say.

"The liberation of queers is about as likely as men walking on the moon, Hekla."

I pull the last page out of the typewriter and place it on the pile, face down. It's page 238. Then I stand up from the table and walk over to him. He looks at me.

"Even if the world can't accommodate a queer, Hekla, it can at least find room for a female writer."

"Let's go to sleep," I say. "You'll feel differently tomorrow."

"Tomorrow is seven minutes away," he says.

Dear Hekla,

We have finally moved to Sogamýri. The neighbourhood is full of half-finished houses with many children inside. We live in the only room that has been completed and I cook on one hotplate in the laundry room. The bathroom, however, has just been covered with yellow tiles. Lýdur did the tiling but I got to choose the colour. We still haven't got the inside doors and there's plastic instead of glass in the living-room windows. Beside us are the open foundations of a building full of yellow water. I'm so scared of Thorgerdur falling into them and I don't let her out of my sight. At the end of the month, I'll be getting a cooker and sink in the kitchen. We're going to lay a lawn next summer and I dream of planting a bush on one side of it—preferably redcurrant—and have a pretty flower bed. I want poppies most of all.

   Your friend,

   ÍSEY

The body of the earth

A bizarre whine resounds, not unlike the howling of an animal or the wailing of wind pressing against a loose windowpane in the heart of winter, and, just as swiftly, the floor of the 400-year-old guest house is jolted and there's a rumble, as if a throng of forty horses had suddenly been unleashed from a bare patch of land and started to gallop. The earth trembles under the foundations, everything is in motion. The wardrobe shifts and I see it fall flat over the bed, the garden rails collapse, the windows shake, a fissure has opened in the earth. There is a cracking sound, like the wall has fractured.

I lie on the grass chewing straw when Mum comes running out.
When we go back inside after the earthquake, the kitchen cupboards
are open and two Bing & Grøndahl porcelain cups with white birds
and gilded rims lie broken on the floor.

I grab the typewriter and manuscript and rush outside.

Hekla dear,

It's been an inclement winter. A heavy snowstorm has now broken
out from the east with a fierce spell of frost. Your brother met a girl at
a Thorrablót feast but it was a short-lived relationship because he got
jilted. It's a long way to the end of wintertide. Surtsey is still erupting.

YOUR FATHER

Dear Hekla,

Thank you for the manuscript. I read it in one session and shut
myself off (I had it in the taxi so I could dive into it between fares).
I was surprised by your request to use my name on the cover of the
book. Nevertheless, I fully understand that you want the book to be
published. At first I thought it was preposterous for me to appropriate
your work, but after careful consideration and consulting my girlfriend
Sædís about it, I am willing to accept your request. The book shall
therefore be mine.

STARKADUR PJETURSSON

NOTES ON QUOTATIONS

There are loose translations from Nietzsche on page 7 and page 191. Loose translations of poems by Hulda are quoted on page 23, Grímur Thomsen on page 122, Steingrímur Thorsteinsson and Jónas Hallgrímsson on page 160, Karítas Thorsteinsdóttir on page 184, and Stephan G. Stephansson on page 209.

The headings on pages 15, 242 and 245 are references to the Song of Songs in the Bible. The heading on page 102 is an indirect reference to Tomas Tranströmer. The heading on page 120 is a reference to André Malraux and the second heading on page 201 to Shakespeare. The headings on the following pages reference lines of poetry by the following authors: on page 143 to Stein Steinarr, page 193 to Abelmajid Benejelloun, the first heading on page 205 to Mhamed Lakira, the second heading on the same page to Haldór Laxness, and page 229 to Hulda.

READING GROUP QUESTIONS

- Living at home with her baby, Ísey wonders '"What would happen if I strolled into the cloud of smoke [in the poet's café] with Thorgerdur in my arms and ordered a cup of coffee? Or walked into an abstract art exhibition in Bogasalur with the pram?"' What do you think would happen if she did? Do you think mothers are excluded from literary and artistic culture?
- Hekla is pestered by one of her customers at the hotel to participate in a beauty contest to become the next Miss Iceland, a contest that she learns is something of a scam. Do you feel that the novel subverts the idea of a "Miss Iceland"?
- Towards the beginning of the novel, Ísey reads Hekla's coffee cup and declares '"There are two men in the cup… You love one and sleep with the other."' The end of the novel finds Hekla married to Jón John, yet the arrangement doesn't seem to make either of them happy. What kind of roles do men and women fulfil in this novel, and does it seem that sex and love between men and women are mutually exclusive?

- The novel is full of other texts that the reader never gets to read, in particular Hekla's many manuscripts both published and unpublished. Was their absence from the novel significant to you? What did you make of the presence of women's voices in the novel?

- Towards the end of the novel, Jón John declares that "Even if the world can't accommodate a queer... it can at least find room for a female writer." How do Jón John and Hekla's experiences of discrimination and oppression, as a gay man and as a woman respectively, compare? How similar are the forces that oppress them?

- Jón John recounts how his mother once told him "When you move abroad to find your roots, you will call yourself D.J. Johnsson". What's in a name for the characters of *Miss Iceland*?